D0330910

ANIANA DEL MAR
JUMPS IN

ANIANA DEL MAR
JUMPS IN

JASMINNE MENDEZ

DIAL BOOKS FOR YOUNG READERS

Dial Books for Young Readers
An imprint of Penguin Random House LLC, New York

First published in the United States of America by Dial Books for Young Readers,
an imprint of Penguin Random House LLC, 2023

Dial & colophon are registered trademarks of Penguin Random House LLC.
The Penguin colophon is a registered trademark of Penguin Books Limited.
Visit us online at PenguinRandomHouse.com.
Library of Congress Cataloging-in-Publication Data is available.
Printed in the USA
ISBN 9780593531815
3rd Printing
BVG
Design by Jennifer Kelly
Text set in Bembo MT Pro

For my tía Morena, who taught me to live and love "con ganas."

For all the imperfect daughters who dare to dream.

For all JIA patients and their families.

"The water we drink, like the air we breathe, is not a part of our body but is our body. What we do to one—to the body, to the water—we do to the other."
—Natalie Diaz

"I wish,
I could be the perfect daughter, but I come back to the water.
No matter how hard I try."
—Moana

CONTENTS

PROLOGUE

WHEN I LEARNED TO SWIM

Before my brother, Matti, is born

before I learn how to keep secrets,

before I learn what my name means
and how it ties me to the water,

Papi teaches me how to swim.

Mami is away in the Dominican Republic
visiting family and friends she hasn't seen in years.

I am six and still afraid of everything.

Papi knows Mami won't like it.
But he decides it's time for me to learn.

THE FIRST TIME

I tremble near the edge of a pool.

My knees KnOcK
                kNoCk
                        KnOcK
against each other.

A warm August wind w h o o s h e s
through my tangled curls,

I almost let go of my Minnie
Mouse towel when—

Papi nudges me
a little closer to the edge.

I   jUmP   back
as if the pool is a sinkhole of blue flames.

I squeal
a high-pitched trumpet tingling my tonsils:

No,
    no,
        no!
I don't want the water
    in my eyes
        in my nose
            in my lungs.
Mami says that the water . . .

Sssh mi reina, no pasa nada.

Papi sits me on his lap,
tells me a cuento para calmarme.

Papi: *The first time I swam*
in the green rivers of el campo,

the current slapped me around
until my arms began to flip

and my legs began to flap
and suddenly I was flying underwater.

Your body will know
how to handle the water

as long as you don't resist it.

JUMPING IN

Papi's big brown arms
wrap around my waist.

His warm breath tickles
my ear and his black beard
sweeps against my cheek.

Papi whispers:
Concentrate—

Reach your arms out, then pull
them apart as if you are parting
the purple curtains in your room.

Kick your legs like a drummer's hands
when they paddle their palms
on a Palo drum.

Imagine your body is a feather
and you'll float. Let the water hold
you. Remember, yo estoy aquí.

He squeezes my hand.

1
    2
       3!
           We jump in.

THE ISLAND (& ME):
May

MY ISLAND

We live on an   island.
The island where we live
is an o u t s t r e t c h e d   arm   reaching
into the Gulf of Mexico.

Galveston:

Where the streets are lined
with papel picado houses
in peacock green and
pomegranate pink.

Hundreds of shotgun houses
where the wind whistles
in through the front door and shoots
directly down the hallways
out the back.

Hundreds of houses
in sherbet colors that remind Mami
of "back home."

But this is the only home
I've ever known.

On Sundays before church,
I like to walk to the seawall,
alone,
and watch the sunrise explode
in the sky like cascarones
on Easter.

Blue, pink, and orange colors
confetti the horizon and kiss the sea.

Sometimes, I don't know.
if the ocean is the sky
or the sky is the ocean.

It opens
        BIG
              W I D E
                      E N D L E S S.

The way I do
when I swim.

Sometimes, I think that if
I swim long enough
I'll reach that cascarón sky
and instead of swimming
I'll begin to S O A R.

WANTS ME CLOSE

Some Sundays
after church, Mami,
Matti, and me
go to the beach.

Sometimes I build
sandcastles with Matti.

Sometimes, if Papi
is with us and goes
in the water with me,
Mami lets me   S W I M.

Mami doesn't like it
that I swim underwater
so far away from her.

I try to tell her:

Papi taught me
how to hold my breath,
stroke my arms,
and kick my fins,
like a dolphin.
I'll be fine.

Still—

shewantsmeclose.

She's afraid la mar
will swallow me up

the way it swallowed
her brother
her house and
her village
during a storm long ago
when she was just a girl.

Mami calls the ocean
"la mar" instead of "el mar"
because she believes
the ocean is a strong woman
who gives and takes life
when she wants.

The ocean will betray you
she says.

I try to tell her:

I am Ani
de las aguas
I swim
with the dolphins.
The water and I
protect each other.
She won't take me
away from you.

Still—

shewantsmeclose.

BIRTH STORY

Mami says when I was born,
I almost drowned
in the ocean of her belly
and they had to C U T me   out.

I was not ready
for the world,
        would not latch,
                    would not eat,
                            would not stop crying.

So they slipped tubes
through my nose
and fed me food
that was not Mami's milk.

Mami says this made her worry
we would not bond
and I would not have enough
of what I needed to grow
big and strong.

And sometimes I worry
she was right.

HOLDS ME CLOSE

A veces Mami mentions
her brother Mateo
and how he was not strong
enough for this world
and now she's afraid
something will happen to me.

And—

some days when el mar's
waves have been wild
and I've swam too much
I get these aches and pains
that pulse in my elbows
and knees, and my hips
and shoulders feel hot
to the touch.

Mami shakes her head
and says: *Ya vez, te lo dije.*
                    La mar es traidora.

Then she rubs Agua Florida
on the places where it aches

And—

sheholdsmeclose.

MONDAYS & WEDNESDAYS

On Mondays and Wednesdays after school,
I spend time with Papi
while Mami and Matti go to church
with las hermanas.

Las hermanas are the women
from Mami's Bible study group
who wear long skirts and carry
la Biblia under their arms.
They always look like they've been crying.
They like to lay their hands over my head.
They try to pray the evil in me away.

Mami makes me go to church on Sundays.
But she doesn't make me
go to church on Mondays and
Wednesdays because Papi
pulled on her heartstrings
with white roses and white chocolate
and he pleaded with words
to convince her to let me come with him.

He said when I was a little girl
the Coast Guard kept sending him away
and he missed important milestones
and he has to make up for lost time.

When he said that, Mami's heart
melted like the chocolate
in Papi's hands and she said:
Okay, okay, okay.

DADDY-DAUGHTER DATES

Papi tells Mami we're going
to the movies or the mall.

We call them "daddy-daughter dates."
But we actually go to the YMCA,

for swim practice and swim meets.
Where Papi watches me

win races, lap after lap, heat after heat.

SWIM PRACTICE

Swimming jiggles
the joints at my
elbows and knees
and shakes
my shoulders
l o o s e.

I prefer salt water
to swimming pools,

but all I want
is to
sLiP
        s l i d e
                D r I f T
                      g l i d e
in gallons
of any kind of water.

13

So I swim laps
in the pool
to practice for my next
Saturday swim meet
and medley.

Backstroke.
    Breaststroke.
        Butterfly.
            Front Crawl.
                Freestyle.

Before I jump in,
me and my teammates
warm up and stretch.

Coach tells me to
keep my legs taut and
my head down.

While Papi keeps time
and holds the timer
like a trophy
he's already won.
His fist flies UP in the air.

Papi: *Go!*
        Go!
            Go!
                That's my girl!

I lift myself out
of the water,
a hungry dolphin

reaching its head out
for a flopping fish.

Me: *How was my time?*

I ask,
hoping I've caught
a big one and beat
my last record.

Papi smiles:
    Your best yet.

BASKETBALL VS. SWIMMING

After practice all the girls
from the team head to
the locker rooms.

We get dressed
and complain about
the chlorine in our
eyes and the armpit smell
in the gym.

While I get dressed,
Maria Tere, my best friend,
stumbles into the locker room
sweaty and out of breath
from basketball practice.

Usually while I'm in the water
swimming laps,

she's on the court
shooting hoops.

She r u n s and steals,
     PiVoTs and t h r o w s.

She crouches and CaTcHeS,
     dribbles and p a s s e s.

Maria Tere doesn't understand
how I can like swimming
so much.

She says she prefers
the solid ground
beneath her feet
to the wishy-washy waves
of the water
and the unsteady motion
of the ocean.

She prefers
the round rubber ball
thick and tight in her grip
because it doesn't slip
through her fingers
like water or sand.

Maria Tere says:
If you are a dolphin,
then I am an oak,
tall and rooted to the earth,
but reaching toward the sky.

MARIA TERE & ME

Maria Tere is not only my best friend
  but also my prima and my "secrets sister."

She's my madrina's daughter.
  We're not really primas. But we are.

We've decided we don't need
  blood to bind us.

Once, when we still played with dolls
  and didn't need shoes or bras just to go outside,

we cut a small clump of our hair
  and made one brown/black braid with our strands.

We buried it in my backyard,
  spat in the soil, and pinky swore

we'd be locked for life. Maria Tere knows
  all my secrets and I know hers.

Once, I found her kissing another
  girl and I didn't tell anyone—
     (not even the water).

PICK ME

Paola and Pilar, the twins
with identical long black
hair and midnight eyes,
pat me on the back
and congratulate me on
breaking my last record
and chatter about
the latest swim team gossip.

Pilar: *I heard Coach Leslie . . .*

Paola: *. . . the one from Elite Swim Camp . . .*

Pilar: *. . . might be here at our next meet!*

Paola: *She wants to recruit girls from our team.*

Me: *Seriously?!*

Paola and Pilar: *YES!*

Me: *She wants some of US to go to Elite Swim Camp?*
The camp where swimmers train
with Olympians and professionals?

Paola and Pilar: *YES!*

They squeal and my heart races
hopeful that if she does come
she'll pick me, me, me.

HIDE THE EVIDENCE

In the locker room
Maria Tere and my
teammates watch me
hide the evidence
of my secret.

The cold chlorinated water
ashes my brown skin
with white dots
and dries me out.

I slather cocoa butter
between the folds of my joints
so Mami won't notice
how the hills and valleys
around my knuckles
and knees CrAcK open.

Paola hands me a tub
of Vaseline and says:

Here, this will do the trick.

Pilar nods in agreement.
*Our skin gets really dry. This is
the only thing that works.*

The silver swim cap
pulls tight against
the nape of my neck
but it never keeps
the water out.

I dry my spongy curls
with a blow-dryer
and a diffuser
that looks like the black-
toothed mouth of a monster
ready to swallow
my head whole.

The hot air blows free
and keeps my curls
from frizzing too much.

D r I p   dRiP   DrIp

Saline burns and softens
the red lines
that web around
my eyes and threaten
to reveal to Mami
what I wish
I could just tell her.

Maria Tere lets me borrow
her tinted moisturizer,
since Mami won't let
me wear makeup yet,
and I dab a few drops
of it on my face where
the goggles pressed
too tight and tattooed
themselves around my
eyes, my forehead,
and the bridge of my nose.

After three months
of training in secret,
with the help of Maria Tere
and my teammates,
I've learned almost all
the tricks I need
to keep Mami from
learning the truth.

I shove my swimsuit
in a plastic bag
and promise myself
I'll remember to toss it
in the dryer after Mami
goes to bed tonight.

PAIN POINT

Swimming and getting changed
wears me out
and makes my body
twinge and ache.

My knee is swollen
to the size of a tennis
ball and it feels hot
when I touch it.

I hobble to a bench and sit,
pull out the elastic
compression wrap
that Coach taught each one of us

how to bind around body parts
that may sprain, ache, or swell.

It pulses a bit
and is tender like a bruised
spot on a piece of rotting fruit.

Maria Tere points
to the bulge in my leg.

Maria Tere: *Yo! What*
happened to your knee?

Me: *I don't know. It happens*
if I swim too much
and mostly when I wake up
in the morning, but then it goes away.
I guess today it's a little
aggravated.

Maria Tere: *Have you shown it*
to your mom or dad?

Me: *No. It eventually goes away.*
It's no big deal.

Paola and Pilar stop
primping their hair
and turn to look at my knee.
They scrunch their noses
and shake their heads.

Paola: *That does NOT*
look fine.

Pilar: *Yeah, you should definitely
get that checked.*

Me: *I'll be fine. It will go away.
It's probably just growing pains.*

I finish wrapping my knee
and throw on my jeans
so everyone can stop staring
at the swelling that until now I thought was normal.

ON THE CAR RIDE HOME

Papi asks me how I feel.
Chlorinated and ready to collapse, I tell him:

Me: *Tired but happy.*

Papi: *Qué bueno. It's good
for your spirit to do the things you love.
I'm glad swimming makes you happy.*

I ask Papi:
*Why do we have to lie to Mami?
Wouldn't she also want me to be happy?*

Papi runs his hands along the steering
wheel and shifts in his seat.

He says: *It's just better this way.
If she knew you were in the water so often
she would worry, worry, worry.
You know she's overprotective of you
and Matti. We will tell her one of these days.*

Me: *But when will that be, Papi?*

Papi: *When you win an Olympic medal.*

Papi winks and I think and dream
about winning medals and meeting
Olympians at Coach Leslie's
swim camp
and I wait for the day when I
can share
all these dreams with Mami.

SHAME

I do not like to
keep secrets from Mami but
the water calls my
name, I listen—the secret
a
     s
      i
        n
          k
            i
              n
                g
                   ship inside me.

FROM MY BEDROOM WINDOW

When we get home from practice
I plop down on my bed.
The sea salt air floats in
through the window
and the last little bit of sun
warms my skin.

I close my eyes and listen
as the house settles and
the ocean sounds wash over me.

OUR HOUSE

Our house is old.
  Our house is historic.
    Our house holds on to sounds
      and silences like a sponge.

Sometimes when Mami and Papi fight,
  over church, the bills, or what's broken
    inside the house or needs to be fixed,

their screams and silent treatment
  get trapped between the wood walls
    and steep steps and sometimes at night I feel
      like the staircase is yelling back at me.

Every time the AC hisses on or the pipes freeze
  and wheeze, I hear the leftovers of Mami's sighs
    when she's sad because the Coast Guard
      has sent Papi away again.

Our house has heavy doors
  that groan "oh! oh! oh!"
    when you open or close them.

When the wind whistles
  and s n a k e s through the windows,
    it leaves a sharp chill in the air
      that slithers under my skin
        and sometimes makes my knuckles ache.

When the wind is strong
  our house shakes itself out,
    sneezes dust bunnies
      burrowed between floorboards

and I hear the memories and the mistakes
        of the people who lived here
                long before we ever moved in.

Our house is the smallest one on the street.
        Three bedrooms, one bathroom.
            Windows that stick and rattle.
                A four-foot porch that juts out
                    like a lonely tooth.

Even though it's small, our shotgun
        house is the prettiest one on the block.
            It's ocean blue with teal shutters, it POPS!
                Like a colorful quinceañera dress at a party.

This time of year, our house is an oasis.
        Mami's marigolds and magnolias
            scent the air with their sweet perfume.

The amaryllis open their red mouths,
        and a ballet of butterflies flit and twirl
            from petals to porch swing every spring.

Our house has an orange tree Papi planted
        the day Mami brought me home from the hospital.
            It hovers and hangs with dozens of fist-sized oranges
                that polka-dot our front yard when they fall to the ground.

Our house is a grandmother
        with achy joints and soft hands.
            She creaks and moans.
                She is serious and slow.
                    She's a secret keeper and a storyteller
                      if you listen closely enough.

BIG SISTER

Just
like it's Mami's job to
protect me, it's my job to protect my
little brother, Matti. He is only four and needs
to learn things I already know. After swim practice,
before dinner we like to sit under the orange tree. He curls
up on my lap while I peel him an orange. My fingers drip with
the tart and tangy juice. I feed him a slice. Matti smacks his lips
and asks for more. I warn him not to swallow the seeds. I've taught
him other things too like: *Remember to blow, blow, blow your food*
before you take a bite. Look left and right before stepping off the sidewalk
into the street. Don't talk to strange people in the park or at the beach.
Pay attention to when the streetlights flicker on so you can find your
way inside before it gets too dark. Watch the rising tide and do not
get too close and do not wade in too far—unless you're a dolphin
like me. Whenever I call myself a dolphin, Matti giggles
and asks, *If you're a dolphin, where are your fins?*
I point to my heart and say,
Right here.

MAMI'S ISLAND

When Mami isn't busy
reading her Bible or
stockpiling cans
and supplies for hurricane season
or banging pots and pans
in the kitchen and cooking,
she joins us under the orange tree.

She sits Matti on her lap,
peels us oranges and tells us
stories about "back home."

When Mami says "back home,"
she means her island—the other   island
in the middle of the Caribbean Sea
and the Atlantic Ocean.
The island she and Papi call
Quisqueya.

Quisqueya is
an island of coconuts,
white sand beaches,
baseball, and Bachata.

It is an island where Spanish
sounds like a saxophone
cut off before the end
of a song.

Quisqueya   Quisqueya   Quisqueya

Mami licks her fingers
and closes her eyes

as if the word and the
sweet tartness of the orange
take her back to some other
time and place.

Quisqueya   *Quisqueya*   *Quisqueya*

She smiles
a smile of a thousand suns
whenever she says it.

I giggle because I think
Quisqueya sounds like
cosquillas.

Quisqueya   *Quisqueya*   *Quisqueya*

When I say it
it sounds like a secret
that tickles the roof
of my mouth
and so I smile too.

BACK HOME

Mami: *Back home*
the sun is hotter
than it is here. It burns
the scalp if you're not
careful.

Back home the ocean
is teal and turquoise,

not brown and muddy
like here.

Back home,
I'm surrounded
by family and music
and bochinche
all the time.

Back home,
I taught my Mateo,
mi hermanito,
how to protect himself.

Matti licks his arm
dripping with orange juice
and asks:
How would you protect him, Mami?

Mami: *We would run in the streets*
barefoot but I taught him
how to watch for glass
and rocks.

We would ride motoconchos,
little motorcycles,
that could fit six or ten
people in one seat, and
I would make Mateo
ride in the middle like a piece
of lunch meat wedged between
our cousins and me.

I wouldn't let him swim
in the river or the sea

because his lungs
weren't strong enough,
so instead I'd let him watch me.
I used to love the water
just as much as you do, Ani.
But then . . .

Mami sighs, strokes my hair,
and hugs Matti closer.

. . . the hurricane came . . .

and I learned I couldn't
protect my Mateo from everything . . .

Mami's voice cuts off
like a phone call
with bad reception,
and I know the conversation
is over because when Mami
mentions Mateo,
the tears always fall
before she's finished her story.

THE END

One day I hope
Mami will tell me
what happened to her
Mateo.

She never tells us
all the details.

I think because it hurts
too much or maybe
because she believes
saying something
out loud makes it real,
and Mami still hasn't
figured out how
to let Mateo go.

FLOOD

Some-
times
Mami
wakes in
the middle
of the night
screaming—
Mateo! Mateo!
Mateo! I'm sorry. I'm
sorry. I'm so sorry—Her
screams F L O O D the halls
of our house like los llantos of
la Llorona and echo in the
walls long after everyone
has fallen back to
sleep.

MARIA TERE AND I DON'T TALK, WE TEXT

Maria Tere: *You going to the Y this Wednesday?*

Me: *Yep*

Maria Tere: *Do you have a meet or just practice?*

Me: *Just practice.*

Maria Tere: *How have you been feeling?*

Me: *Fine. Y?*

Maria Tere: *Last week after the meet, you said you were sore . . .*

Me: *I'm fine now . . .*

Maria Tere: *But how's your knee? It was really swollen.*

Me: *It's FINE Dr. Tere.*

Maria Tere: *haha*

Me: *Don't worry so much. The swelling is almost gone.*

Maria Tere: *When's your next meet?*

Me: *Saturday.*

Maria Tere: *Is your mom gonna come?*

Me: *When's your next game?*

Maria Tere: *Monday. You didn't answer my question.*

Me: . . .

Maria Tere: *You haven't told her yet have you?*

Me: *Papi says we'll tell her soon.*

Maria Tere: *You're never gonna tell her.*

Me: *Are YOU ever gonna tell YOUR mom about that time you kissed a girl?*

Maria Tere: *She already knows.*

Me: *What? She does?*

Maria Tere: *Yes. Not all of us have to keep secrets from our mothers.*

JEALOUSY

Sometimes, I admit,
I am jealous
of Maria Tere, and

I wish Madrina
was my mom too because she
always listens to

and understands me.
Madrina does not judge or
try to change me. She

is a cool mom who
hasn't forgotten what it's
like to be us. But,

Maria Tere says
she is jealous of me 'cause
my dad didn't leave

us when I was born
like hers did. Wishes her dad
was part of her life.

Says she tried to reach
out to him but he told her
to leave him alone.

That makes me sad for
her. But maybe no parent
is better than a mean one.

SATURDAY

The Saturday swim meet
is early and will last all day.

Papi tells Mami he's going
to take me fishing

for a special daddy-daughter date.
Mami says okay.

Because she's sending Matti
to spend the day with Madrina,

and she's looking forward to
cleaning the whole house

without any of us
in her way.

SWIM MEET

While I wait
                and wait
                        and wait

for my turn to hit
the starting block,
I sit in the stands
with Paola and Pilar
and we play Uno
and listen to music.

Some girls write
or draw on their
arms in permanent
marker for fun.

Some girls gossip
or gush about boys
on the basketball
and soccer teams.

Sometimes I join
in and draw, or talk
if I have something
to say.

But today I decide
to be alone and get
in the zone before
I hit the water,

because if what Paola and Pilar
said is true, Coach Leslie
might be at this meet today
and I want to do my best.

I shake out my nerves,
and focus on breathing.
Stretch out my arms
and shoulders and hum
a song or two.

When the referee finally
blows the short whistle
I walk up next to
my starting block.

I hear Papi and Maria Tere
screaming my name.

The referee blows
the long whistle and
I stand on my block.

I take my mark.

My feet grip the rubber.
The starter signals and
the horn blows
and I'm
          O   F   F!

IN THE WATER

When I'm in the water
I feel weightless,
calm and free.

I focus on the black
line and the pulse
of my heart
pounding inside me.

When I'm in the water
time slows down
and nothing else matters.

When I'm in the water
I know it's exactly
where I want and need
to be.

AFTER THE MEET

Papi hugs me even though
I'm soaking wet.
He holds my medal
for winning the 100 relay
and presses it against his chest.

Papi: *That was wonderful, Ani!*
The way you glide in the water!
Your speed! Your stroke!
It's perfection!
I'm so proud of you!

Me: *Does that mean we can tell Mami now?*

Papi hands me my towel,
I grip it close to my chest.
My heart thump, thump
thumps fast from my relay
and from the possibility
that Papi will say yes.
But instead,
he sighs and shakes his head.
No.

My heart sinks and slips
to the bottom of my stomach.
I wring the towel in my hands
and wipe my face now wet
with chlorine and tears.

Me: *But I want her to come to my next meet!*
I want her to see me win my heats!

Papi lifts my medal up and it
catches the light.
It shimmers and spins around.
Papi smiles.

Papi: *Ay Ani. Let's enjoy this moment.*
We can talk about all that later.

Me: *Pero Papi . . .*

He throws one hand up
as if to silence me
as if to say "enough."

Papi: *Mami sufre de los nervios.*
You know that. And you know how
she gets this time of year. Hurricane
season starts in June and she's a wreck because . . .

Papi waves his arms in the air flustered.
My medal falls to the ground,
and his voice trails off.

Me: *Because of her brother . . .*

Papi: *Yes. So you see, that's why we can't*
tell her NOW. This is the way it has to be.
I'll tell her when I'm ready. At the right time.

He picks up my medal
and places it around my neck.
It's cold and heavy against my chest.
I shiver and wonder if winning
would feel better if Mami were around
to witness it.

READY

I don't know when
Papi will feel "ready"
to tell Mami.
But until that time comes,
we will keep our secret
and I know when we get home,
Papi will hide my medal
in his toolbox in the garage
with the others
because he knows
Mami will never
find them there.

SEARCH

When Papi and me walk in
through the front door,
Mami is at the stove.

Her eyes and arms
watch and stir
a blue and white
polka-dotted pot
bubbling and steaming
a savory song
of arroz con pollo.

Mami: *Did you catch a lot of fish?*

Me: *No.*   **Papi**: *Yes.*

Mami: *Hmmmm*

My tongue moves quick
like a jumping jellyfish.

Me: *We did catch a lot but I made Papi put them back.*

Mami: *How many did you catch?*

Me: *Three.*   **Papi:** *Five.*

Mami's head turns up,
her forehead wet with sweat.

Me: *I guess I lost count.*

Mami: *Hmmmmm.*

Mami's curls limp and sway
in   S   waves
against her damp cheek.

She   . tAp   TaP   tApS
the wooden rice spoon
on the edge of the pot
and walks toward me.

She cups the crown of my head,
kisses the heart-shaped mole
on my right temple,
and whispers in my ear:

Mami: *Your hair is damp . . .*
Truthful lips endure forever,
a lying tongue is but for a moment.

Mami always quotes
the Bible when she wants
to shame me about something.

Her eyes tiptoe around
my face in search of
an answer.

Her gaze is a black flame
burning h o l e s
into my brown skin.

I search the kitchen
for Papi, but he has left
the room.

He probably went to hide
my medal, but why would he leave
me alone   an island
in the middle of Mami's
impending hurricane?

Or maybe he's mad at me
because I want to tell Mami the truth
and he doesn't?

I swallow the conch
shell in my throat.

Mami: *WHERE did you go today?*

Mami TaP   tAp   TaPs
the wooden spoon.
A single curl hangs between
her brows, a (?)
I do not want to answer.

AND RESCUE

Where did you go today?

Dance with me,
Papi says as he prances
back into the room
like a welcome wind
on a steamy August day.

He pulls Mami away
from me and winks
from behind the ocean
of her salt-and-pepper waves.

A slow Bachata bounces
out of the speakers.

Where did you go today?

Mami is not supposed
to dance, according to
the rules of the church.
But when Papi asks her
Mami can never say no.

Papi thinks dancing
with Mami will help her
forget what we were
talking about.

But I still hear her question
ringing in the air
around us like a wind chime
or a warning.

Where did you go today?

OCEAN & MOON

Madrina
once told
me that
the ocean
is led by
the waxing
and waning
of the moon.
If that's true,
then Mami's
the ocean and
Papi is her
full moon.

BEHIND CLOSED DOORS

But even the ocean
can't be tamed by the moon.

Later that night,
when Mami and Papi think
me and Matti are sleeping
they close the door
and fight.

Their voices echo
between
the cracks in the wall,
and scurry down the hall
into my room, where I
can hear every other
word.

Pool—
    Lied!
Swimming—
    Dangerous!
Cálmate—
    Not safe!

Doors open and slam.
My bedroom floor shakes.

I turn out my light
and wait for sleep to find me.
I hate that my secret
is the reason Mami and Papi
are fighting.

WHEN SLEEP DOESN'T COME, I TEXT

Me: *Mami knows*

Maria Tere: *About what?*

Me: *Swim team!*

Maria Tere: *But how?!*

Me: *I'm pretty sure Papi told her, they just had a huge fight*

Maria Tere: *What r u gonna do?*

Me: *Jump in the ocean*
  and live with the dolphins,
        I guess

FEELS BAD

The next morning
Matti and me
get ready for church.

Mami stomps around
the house not speaking
to anyone but yelling
out into the halls
about everything:

Where are my keys?!
    Why is everything a mess?!
        ¡Tengo que hacerlo todo yo sola!

Papi shuffles around upstairs
and quietly gets ready too.

Maybe it's because he feels
bad about their fight last night.
Maybe it's because it's Mother's
Day AND he feels bad about
their fight last night.

SILENT APOLOGIES

Papi doesn't usually come
with us to church on Sundays
because Papi is Catholic
and he says church should
only last one hour and not
all day.

Papi also says we show God
we love him by what we do
every day and not just on Sundays.

Mami always invites Papi
to church and Papi almost always
says no.

Mami doesn't try to force
him because she says:

*Your father is a grown man
and I can't make him do anything.*

But when Mami doesn't ask
Papi to come it means she's mad
at him and that's when Papi
puts on a white shirt and
blue slacks and gets in the car.

It's his way of saying
"I'm sorry"
without actually saying it.

MOTHER'S DAY

After church Papi insists
we take Mami to her favorite
restaurant on the seawall
for tacos and a virgin margarita.

Mami never says no to tacos
from Tortuga's, so we go
and we sit on the deck facing
the ocean and I close my eyes
and listen to her song.

Before our entrée arrives,
I munch on chips and finish almost
the whole bowl of queso
by myself while Matti colors
on the kid's menu.

When Papi returns from a
"quick trip to the car," he's holding
a pink-and-yellow striped gift bag
in his hands.

This is another silent apology.
An apology Mami is happy to accept.

Her eyes light up and she
shimmies her shoulders.
She pulls out a blue-and-pink paisley
patterned Bible cover that has her initials
embroidered on the front:

P.M.D.

Papi points to the letters:
P.M.D. *Your initials.*
Patria Mercedes del Mar.

I nudge Papi on the elbow
and say
Thank you, Capitan Obvious.

Mami chuckles and nods.
Matti pulls the cover out
of Mami's hands to see.

As a cool "not yet summer" breeze
blows by and blends with
the ocean's song, I make a wish:

I wish this moment could last
forever.

MORE DOORS CLOSED

Monday,
when we arrive at the Y
for swim practice
and a sign on the door
says:

POOL CLOSED
FOR REPAIRS

I ask Papi to take me
to the beach instead.

I never did find out
if Coach Leslie was at
the swim meet.

But camp or no camp,
Mami or no Mami,
I'm determined
to keep swimming
no matter how many
doors close in my face.

TOURISTS

In Texas, May marks
the unofficial beginning
of summer, which means
college students
and tourists
from other Texas towns
crowd the beach
and take up too much

S p A c E

on the seawall
and in the streets.

The tourists love
to DuMp trash
and talk trash
while lounging
on the sandy beaches
of my island.

Gaaaalvessston
they say, and wrinkle
their noses as if
ga-ga-ga-gagging
on the gallons of gray
smoke that fill the sky
from the power plants
nearby.

They edge near the water
as if afraid to get in.

They're disappointed
they're not near
blue-green waves like
the ones they might find
on Mami's island.

Galveston's water
looks brown because
the Mississippi River empties
itself out into the Gulf
and all the mud settles here.
But the tourists don't
care about the truth.
They just complain
and criticize:

Oh my GaWd
the water is SO gross.

They moan and groan.
They tiptoe into an ocean wave
and leave more
than just f o o t p r i n t s
behind in the sand.

GODDESS

I don't care what they say.
I love my island.
I think Galveston is a gallant
Greek goddess who holds history
inside her sea-walled feet
and palm-tree hands.
I know she is strong
because she is able to survive
storm surges and sea sickness
year
            after year
                        after year.

A SAFE PLACE TO HIDE

Papi drives down the seawall
but doesn't stop because
we like pocket beaches best.

Papi likes pocket beaches best
because he can drive right up
to the shore with his car
and park right in front
of the water—No stairs
                    to walk down.
             No struggling
                    to find a spot in the sand
                           to sit or sunbathe.
             No parking meter app to pay
                    or program on your phone.

I like pocket beaches best
because they remind me
of the scaly seashells
I like to collect and hold
in my hands—their mouths
                    a secret place
             to hide sand
                    and seawater.

We like pocket beaches best
because most tourists don't
come here.
Because out here—
there's nothing to do for fun
(except the water).

And lucky for us
that's all we need.

MADRE DE LAS AGUAS

When we arrive at the pocket beach
                on the west end of the island,
                        the ocean is an angry woman
                                singing loud songs about revenge
                                        and betrayal.
                                She thrashes about and feels
                        warmer than she should
                this time of year.
        Papi picks up a plastic
Lunchables tray someone left
        behind in the sand and sighs.
                Papi is in the Coast Guard
                        and believes it his duty
                                to keep our waters safe
                                        from everything
                                                like storms and terrorists,
                                                        like pollution and plastic.
                                                White foam skims and retreats,
                                        kisses and caresses
                                our toes in the sand.
                        Even though I'm almost thirteen
                and have sprouted into a taller,
        bra-wearing version of myself,
my feet look like tiny turtle toes
        next to Papi's large lion paws.
                Papi protests: *This plastic
                        is polluting our water.*
                                Water is life and we owe
                                        everything to her.
                                                I ask Papi: *Have you always*
                                                        loved the water?
                                                I have, he says, *and*
                                        so have you. Papi's eyes
                                sparkle like the sun
                        setting on the sea.

61

COASTIE

A few times a year
Papi sails the sea
on a Coast Guard cutter.

Sometimes he leaves
just for one week.
Sometimes he leaves
for one month or more.

On deck,
with the sun in his face,
and the island to his back,
is when he says
he feels the most
free.

Papi loves being in
or on
or near the water
just as much as I do.

He says our blood is
made of salt water,
our bones are
made of sand,
and our memories are
made of and left behind in
        a breaststroke
                    a backstroke
                            or wake of a boat.

PAPI REMEMBERS:

When you were first born
I brought you to the ocean
so she could bless you.

When I dipped your toes
in the water, the waves got
wilder and faster.

It was like she knew you
would love her and she would
love you just as much.

You were little then.
But even so, you were strong.
You were born fighting.

You were born to be in
the water just like me,
to protect and serve.

ORIGIN

Papi: *Have I ever told you*
     the origin of your name?

Me: *Yes, but tell it again.*

Papi: *You are named after Aniana Vargas.*
          -La madre de las aguas-

She was a fighter,
    water warrior,
        protector of the Earth.

She battled tyrants and terrible men
    with her words and her
        unwavering willpower.

You will grow up to be
    just as strong,
        smart, and special
            as her.

Papi rubs my head with
    his sand–sprinkled hand
        and bends down to pick
            up another piece of plastic.

He exhales
    sorrowfully
        like the sea.

PAPI EXPLAINS

Me: *What's wrong, Papi?*
Are you sad about the beach?

Papi: *No. It's something else.*
I know you heard me
and Mami fighting last week,
and it's all my fault.

It seems I have made
a mess of our secret.
I started to tell

your mother about
swim team and swim meets,
but she got so mad

when I mentioned it
that I told another lie
and said you were just

trying out. I know
it was wrong to lie again,
but she is fragile.

Sometimes, you know,
she gets really sad for weeks
and I don't want that.

Papi's eyes drift off
again, and he hugs me close.

He says: *I'll fix this.*
Go swim—the water has calmed.

LA MAR

I don't ask
        Papi how   I JUMP!
            he will   la mar, so
                fix it because   like I trust
                      I trust him

In the warm
        May water I
            DART   and SWISH!
              and D a N c E   that shuffle
                     between waves

I hear Papi's voice
      in the murmur
           of the ocean's song: and G L I D E.
              Watch your form.   I close my eyes
                Long arms. Strong core.

Salt water
        blesses   *WISH.*
          my sun-kissed   *Make a WISH, WISH,*
              skin clean.   over me, chanting:
                 The water washes

And
      so
          I
             do.

UN DESEO

I wish that Mami
could understand that water
is my church and when
I swim it is like having
a conversation with God.

THE TIN (WO)MAN

The day after swimming on
the beach with Papi, I wake up
statue stiff as if I were made
of marble or stone.

When I wake, my feet
fail to find the floor
and I fumble and
f
a
l
l.

I limp around my bedroom
like a rusty robot.
I creak and stumble
to the bathroom
to brush my teeth.
I trip over my own toes,
and Tin Man my way
through my morning
routine.

This feels like the worst
it's ever been.
I decide to take a hot
shower to help oil
my body back
to normal again.

MORE SECRETS

I do not tell Mami
about my worsening
Tin Man mornings
because
I do not want her
to worry,
or send me to church
to pray it away.

I do not tell Papi
about my clumsy feet
and weak knees
because he thinks
I am strong
and I do not want
to disappoint him.

I decide to tell Madrina
because I know
she will help me
find a remedy.

MAMI AND MADRINA HAVE

brown skin   and
midnight eyes

mountains of curls   and
wide hips

a loud laugh   and
soft hands.

Mami   and
Madrina

are   almost
the same   except,

Mami meanders   and
Madrina skips.

Mami hums   and
Madrina sings.

Mami shouts   and
Madrina listens.

Mami glows   and
Madrina glitters.

Mami prays   and
Madrina heals.

BELIEVERS

Mami and Madrina grew up
together en el campo near the hills.
They bathed juntas in the river,

and ran to the colmado
for frio frios and refrescos
when the island days were too hot

to run in the sun or jump rope.
They were next-door neighbors
who became best friends for life.

They were raised almost exactly
the same but they grew up
to believe in different things.

REMEDIES

Madrina believes in remedies
that Mami does not believe in.

Madrina lights candles
and burns a palo santo stick
to clean our casas and cuerpos
of las cosas malas.

Madrina builds altars
for our ancestors
and strokes stones
between her fingers
to balance and heal
the hurt in her heart.

She wears a stack
of small beaded necklaces
around her neck that she won't
let anyone else touch.
And once a month she pours honey
or molasses into the ocean.

I sometimes think
Madrina's remedies
are like magic tricks
or spells cast by a witch
and I'm not sure they work
but she heals people
with things they can hold
and that feel more real
than Mami's quiet prayers.

"NO HAIR ON HER TONGUE"

Mami may believe in God
and Madrina may believe in goddesses,
but they both believe in each other.

And Mami knows Madrina says
what she says and does what she does
out of love because Madrina has always

picked up the pieces when Mami's
sadness cracks her like a glass vase
and no one, not even Papi, knows

how to fix Mami like Madrina.
Madrina knows how to listen
and always knows what to say.

Papi says: *Tu madrina
no tiene pelos en la lengua.*
Which means Madrina says

what she means and means
what she says. And Mami needs
someone like that in her life

because Madrina is the only
person who doesn't treat Mami
like she is always about to break.

WHEN I WAS BAPTIZED

Madrina says
she let my baby
pink hand squeeze her finger
until it turned
baby blue,
and when the priest
anointed my head
and christened me clean
she summoned spirits
and whispered
in my ear:

This will not be
> *the water*
>> *that saves you.*

THE STRAND

Madrina owns a gift shop
on the Strand—
a section of town
that looks like
a French village
no one around here could
ever afford to visit.

The tourists walk
and shop
along the cobblestone
streets of the Strand
to pretend they're not
in Texas.
To pretend they have
money
to visit a place like Paris.

Each store has its own
personality
and most of them sell
souvenirs,
trinkets and costume
jewelry, novelty
T-shirts, seashell
necklaces, and tie-dye
shorts,
DON'T MESS WITH TEXAS
towels and caps,
and monogrammed
mugs and makeup bags.

CRYSTALS AND CALLIGRAPHY

Madrina's shop is called
Crystals and Calligraphy.

She sells crystals
that promise to heal
and soothe your stress,
your sadness,
and all your inner aches
and pains.

She also sells coffee
and one-of-a-kind
calligraphy pens
and stacks of stationery
made from organic
and recycled paper.

In the back half
of Madrina's shop
is a small café
with rustic tables
and antique chairs.

Sometimes
Maria Tere and I
wipe down counters
and work the register.

Sometimes
Maria Tere and I
sit in the back of the café
and sip on Madrina's

famous Dominican coffee
and guess how much
the white-haired
white women
browsing in Madrina's shop
will spend on crystals
and calligraphy pens.

Madrina insists
she isn't just selling
overpriced stones
and stationery.

Madrina says
she's selling hope
and human connection.

Something
everyone wants
and needs.

STONES & SILENCE

One afternoon while Maria Tere
and I are cleaning counters
in the café, I ask Madrina
if she can keep a secret.

She winks:

I won't say a word.
Pero, if your mami or papi ask
I will tell them the truth.
¿Entiendes?

I nod.
That's good enough for me.
I ask her which stones will silence
the rigid racket under my skin
and bones.

Maria Tere also tells her about
the swelling in my knee.

Madrina stops sweeping under
the table and her eyes squint
curious and concerned.

Madrina: *How and where else does it hurt?*
Sometimes, our ancestors are trying
to speak to us through our bodies.

I point to my knees, elbows,
hips, and hands.

Me: *Sometimes, in the morning*
everything aches.

She walks behind the blue
curtain in the back of the shop
and returns with a velvet purple
pouch.

She pulls out a seaweed-green
stone and places it in my palm.

Madrina: *This is malachite.*
It will ease your morning aches.

Then she carefully lifts a bright
blue stone in front of her face
as if she's plucked a puzzle piece
out of the sky and wants me
to have it.

Madrina: *And this is . . .*

Me: *Laaarrriiimaaarrr . . .*

I whisper, stretching out
each of the vowels in the word
as if it were expensive silk,
as if the word itself were a secret.

Madrina: *Yes, this is the stone of our Quisqueya.*
The stone of our ancestors.
Take this one too.

Larimar will open your throat
　　so the sinking ships in your belly
　　　　can finally rise to the surface and sing.
　　　　　　A girl your age shouldn't have to
　　　　　　　　keep so many secrets.

Now, these crystals are not a cure-all,
　　but if you believe and if you let them,
　　　　they can provide clarity, and help
　　　　　　you on your healing journey.

And remember, when we hold things inside—
　　things that don't belong there—
　　　　the body will always find a way
　　　　　　to spit them back out.

FAITH, OR I DON'T KNOW HOW MADRINA KNOWS ABOUT THE SINKING SHIP IN MY BELLY

I carry the stones
in my pocket and rub them
again and again.
But I also pray like my
mami taught me—just in case.

CATEGORY 1:
(HURRICANE) SEASON

June

MAMI-DAUGHTER DATE

I don't know if Papi ever
"fixed" what he said he was
going to "fix" between him
and Mami because no one
ever really tells me anything.

But Mami seems to be in a better mood.
And on her birthday weekend
she decides she wants to
celebrate her day with ME!

Mami: *Vamos tú y yo*
on a mami-daughter date.
We need girl time.

She doesn't tell me right away
where we're going or what
we're going to do.
She just tells me to grab
her cartera and wear flip-flops
because we're getting a special treat.

We leave Papi and Matti
watching cartoons on the couch.
We hop in the car and no matter
how many times I ask:
Where are we going? What
are we going to do? Tell me!

Mami doesn't respond. She just
smiles like she's breaking a rule
she knows she can get away with.

MY FIRST PEDICURE

When we arrive at Bella Nails and Spa
I squeal because I've never had a pedicure before.

Maria Tere and I are always painting our toes
and playing with makeup but I've never had

a PROFESSIONAL pedicure before and now
I'm wondering if it's going to tickle or hurt.

Mami doesn't paint her nails or toes either because
even though it's not against the rules at church,

Mami knows las hermanas would judge her for it.
Today she says we can paint our toes because

it's her birthday and she can cover her feet with shoes
and socks and las hermanas won't know.

Las hermanas judge everyone for everything even though
I *know* the Bible says "Do not judge thy neighbor."

Mami hugs me as we get inside and giggles like me
and Maria Tere do when we sneak texts in class.

Mami: *Do you like your surprise?*

Me: *Yes! But why am I the one getting a surprise?*
It's YOUR birthday. I should be getting you a gift.

Mami: *Ay, mi'ja, you and Matti are the best gifts*
I've ever received. And seeing you this happy

makes me the happiest mami in all the island.
Now go pick a color, but make sure it's not

red, and that it's not too dark! You're still a little girl,
y esos son colores de mujeres.

Mami picks a pink so pale you'll barely be able to see it.
I pick a light blue polish called ocean shimmer.

BABY BLUES

Mami did not always go to a very religious church.
Mami did not always pray every day or wear long black skirts.
Mami and me used to play, jump rope, and have lots of fun.
Mami and me used pick and plant flowers in the summer sun.

Before Matti was born, we'd cook together and paint.
After Matti was born she didn't have the energy to play games.
When Matti was born, I was already eight.
After Matti was born, Mami wouldn't eat and she lost a lot of weight.

For months and months Mami cried a river of tears.
For months not even Madrina could rid Mami of her fears.
Mami didn't like to leave Matti alone in his crib.
Mami was terrified of something she and Papi called SIDS.

Then one day, when Mami was crying into a pot on the stove,
one day after Papi had gone off to sea and we were home alone,
four women in brown shirts and black skirts knocked on our door.
Four women asked Mami if she had accepted Jesus as her savior.

Mami let them in and served them coffee and pan dulce.
Mami told them all about her sorrows and they said *no se preocupe*.
When Mami joined that Christian church, she became someone new.
After a few weeks of prayer and pan, Mami said she was free of the
baby blues.

SUMMER PLANS

While Mami and I get
our toes pampered and
painted she asks me
about the end of the
school year and where
do I want to go
for summer camp.

She wants me to join
the youth group at church
and be a part of summer
Bible study.

But I tell her I want
to do the sports camp
at the Y.
I don't mention
anything about swimming.

She says there's still time
to decide and as the woman
at her feet begins
to massage her legs with
a hot stone, Mami
closes her eyes and
hums.

I don't know if I've ever
seen her so serene.

GIRL TALK

Me: *Mami, thank you for bringing*
me here today. Happy birthday.
I love you.

Mami opens her eyes
and says: *I love you too.*
And you know everything
I do is to protect you because
I love you, right?

Me: *I know.*

Mami: *And I know Papi took*
you to try out for that swim team
and I know swimming makes you
happy. But you have to understand
that I worry about you.
You were born so small and
so weak. And I know you're stronger
now. But I still worry
that what happened to my Mateo
will happen to you.

I want to tell Mami that it
wasn't a tryout and that I'm actually
already on the swim team.

But I don't,
because I don't want Mami
to get mad

and I don't want Papi
to get mad
and I don't want to mess up
this moment between us.

ON THE WAY HOME

In the car,
still thinking about Mami's
Mateo and hoping she is still
in a sharing mood,
I find the courage to ask her:

What DID happen to Mateo?
I think I'm old enough to understand.
Will you tell me?

Mami shakes her head
and sighs:

What happened was a tragedy, mi'ja.
And it was all my fault.

MAMI'S MATEO

Usually when I ask about
Mami's twin brother, Mateo,
her mouth closes like a gate
to a forbidden place
I am not allowed to enter.

She crosses her arms
in front of her chest
as if to keep her sorrows in
and my questions out.

But not today.

Maybe it's because
it's her birthday and she
just got her feet rubbed
and she's feeling "open
and relaxed," as Madrina would say.

Maybe Mateo is her sinking
ship and she's just tired
of holding it all in.

Whatever the reason,
today Mami opens
her arms and her mouth
and maybe even her heart
and she lets the secret
that has been sinking
in her own stomach
out
    out
        out.

TURTLE SHELL

Mami
says she
and Mateo
were like
a sea
turtle—   different parts belonging to   one body.
Mateo was the soft squishy center that needed protecting,
and she was supposed to be his shell. *Mateo*, she says, *was born*
with   *water in his lungs. Because*, she says, *Grandma had*   *too*
much water in her womb when she pushed him out
into the world. And so for the rest of his short life,
he always found it harder to breathe. So Mami used
her lungs for them both. She would run races and
Mateo would watch. Mateo would skip rocks in
the river and she would fish them out. Mami
would jump and catch fireflies with her hands
and Mateo would save them in a jar.
Mami and Mateo were like different
parts of the same person. And
when Mateo died, Mami
became   an empty turtle shell   crowded
with   a darkness that no light or   love
could   fix or fill ever   again.

HURRICANE GEORGES

Mami says Hurricane Georges
      came   and   C O N Q U E R E D
         S U R G E D and   S W E P T.
               Georges saw what it wanted
                 was the island
                     so it H O V E R E D
               for one, two, three
         four, five
     six, seven, eight
  nine, ten
H   O   U   R   S
   as if trying to rid the ocean
     of all its water.
             Mudslides PUNCHED and PLUNDERED
               tin roof homes.
                   Floods spilled and S W A L L O W E D
               Mami's casita en el campo.
        They tried to outrun
     and outswim its fury.
    Mami R   E   A   C   H   E   D
  for Mateo's hand in the dark
only to grab hold of the night.
  She heard his
     W   H   E   E   Z   I   N   G
    and heavy breathing.
      Saw his arms F L A I L I N G
      like a fish.
          But the current kept
           P U S H I N G
          him away and
              A   W   A   Y

and

A   W   A   Y

until it seemed like all

the water in the world

P O U R E D

into his body and

filled his lungs

with fluid once again.

And there was nothing

Mami could do

to make it

S   T   O   P .

UNDERSTANDING

We get home and sit
in the car in the driveway,
with nothing left to say.

Mami's tears flow like
the water that swallowed her
home and her brother.

Mami's legs shake and
her voice quakes when she says:
He died. It was my fault.

I understand now
why Mami won't let me swim
and why she's afraid

of deep water and
why she believes la mar
should not be trusted.

I understand now
why Papi won't tell Mami
I'm on the swim team

and why he believes
it has to be kept secret.
Why he makes me wait.

I understand now
that Papi is trying to
be her turtle shell.

PEACE

The week after Mami's
birthday, she goes on
an overnight retreat with
las hermanas.

They go to a cabin
in the woods with no
access to technology or
their families and they pray
for hours and hours a day.

They study the Bible,
knit blankets for orphaned
children in other countries
and talk about how to be
good Christian women.

Mami says it's a time when
she feels most at peace
because she doesn't have to
take care of anyone else.

It's a time when I feel
at peace because I don't
have to lie about going
to my swim meet.

INDIVIDUAL MEDLEY

Maria Tere,
Papi,
and my teammates
Paola and Pilar
jump in the stands
and sing and scream
my name:

Ani!   *Ani!*   *Ani!*

Fifty-meter heats:

Butterfly
      Backstroke
                  Breaststroke
                              Free

I win them all.

Dripping wet,
shoulders sore,
triceps and biceps
trembling,
I walk toward the stands,
and my legs wiggle
and jiggle
like Jell-O.

I feel tired but triumphant.

Papi wraps me up
in a warm hug and a towel.

Maria Tere and
my teammates pummel me
with hugs and high fives.

And even though I know
it's not possible,
their claps and squeals
are a melodious melody
I wish Mami were here
to sing too.

SWELL

The day after
the swim meet,
my skin swells
red
and I cannot
get out of
bed.

FEVER DREAM

a fire burns   between my bones   m o l t en magma
          ready to BuRsT

                                        from beneath the sea of me
     for four days   I lie in bed   ShAkE   and curl up
inside my muscles

                    a manic merengue   that won't stop
          STOMPING   and   SHOUTING   a flurry of hands
and heads   hover over my eyes   like Galveston fog

          Mami prays and PaT   pAt   PaTs   my head
                                        with an ice-cold washcloth
my body a warming planet   melting glaciers   Mami tells me to
                                                            drink

                                                  drink

                                        drink
and she floods me
                    with fluids
                              my lips get wet   but my tongue   sticks
to the roof   of my mouth   I am a drought   waiting for rain

I shiver and   Madrina enters   a blur of shadows
          M O O O A A A N N N N
and sage smoke   her chant   floats over me
               my knees   hips and elbows
          b i l l ow   B U L G E   I am the island
                    and   my body the storm

          like a bowl of concrete   in a bed of sand   I
                                                            s

                                                       i

                                                       n

                                                       k

          and try   to dream   of water

NOT WORKING

Mami's praying hands,
    Madrina's magic rocks, and
        Papi's pain medicine
            are not working.

I still cannot
    get out of bed
        without f
             a
              l
               l
                i
                 n
                  g.

I still cannot
    stretch my muscles
        without   w r I t h I n g
                in   p a i n!

BEYOND MY BEDROOM DOOR PART I

Mami: *What did you do while I was gone?*

                                 Papi: *Nothing.*

Mami: *Did you take her swimming again?*

                                 Papi: *No.*

Mami: *Are you lying to me?*

                          Papi: *What does it matter?*

Mami: *Of course it matters.*

                  Papi: *No, what matters is making her better.*

Mami: *What matters is the truth!*

                       Papi: *I'm not doing this right now.*

Mami: *Don't you see?*
   God is punishing her for your secrets and lies!

                             Papi: *¡Ay! ¡Por favor!*
                           That is NOT how God works!

               Doors s L a M!

Mami stomp
        stomp
            stomps
    down the stairs.

                          Papi stomp
                      stomp
                  stomps
                        into his bedroom.

BEYOND MY BEDROOM DOOR PART II

Mami and Papi mumble
about "what to do" and "why her"
and "how did it get so bad?"

Mami yells at Matti to turn
off the TV and go play
outside.

Mami and Madrina hiss
and whisper about the stones
in my pocket and why Madrina
didn't say something sooner.

Madrina feels sorry, so she cooks
and leaves.

Papi wants to save me, so he paces
and paces.

Mami gets mad, then sad, so she cries
and prays.

SOBS & SICKNESS

Papi becomes impatient.

His voice waxes: *Patty!*
then wanes: *She needs medicine, not a miracle.*

Mami sniffles like a puddle
of sea foam collecting quietly
on the ocean shore:

You know how I feel about
doctors and hospitals.

They always find something wrong.
They always only tell you bad news.

What if . . .
    What if . . .

Her words pop
                pop
                    pop
into sobs that soak Papi's shirt
with salt water and sadness.

While I drown in blankets and
pillows wet with sweat and
a sickness no one seems to know
how to cure.

AN APPOINTMENT

Two days later, in the hall
outside my bedroom, Mami
and Papi argue again.

Papi: *I called the pediatrician
and I made an appointment.*

                    Mami: *You made an appointment?*

Papi: *Yes. I made an appointment,
and you're going to take her.*

                    Mami: *You're not going with us?*

Papi: *Yes, but I will be late.
I have to work.*

                    Mami: *I wish you'd cancel it.*

Papi: *I'm not going to cancel it.*

                    Mami: *If you want her to see a doctor,
then you can take her.*

Papi: *Don't you want her to get better?*

                    Mami: *Of course. But you should have asked
me BEFORE making the appointment!*

Papi: *I knew you would say no. When I get there,
if you want, you can leave.*

                    Mami: *No, I will go and I will stay because
I am her mother, but if it were up to me
there would be no appointment.*

IN THE WAITING ROOM

Mami presses her palms
together in prayer position
and paces

               back   and   forth
               back   and   forth.

                                     Her worry a quiet wind
                                     picking up speed, ready
                                     to blow us all away.

I AM THE PATIENT, BUT . . .

If Papi were here
he would tell Mami
to be patient.

If Papi were here
he would tell Mami
to sit down.

If Papi were here
he would tell Mami
it's going to be okay.

Papi should be here
but he's not yet and Mami
and I are losing

our patience.

DR. GREENE AND ME

Dr. Greene's Pepto-Bismol–pink
scrubs match her Pepto-pink
lips and nails.

Her wrists linger with lavender
like the flower oils in Madrina's shop.

Her scent collides with the sharp
smell of rubbing alcohol
in the room.

I GaG.

The white scratchy paper beneath
my thighs rustles and sticks
to the hair on my "too young
to shave" legs.

The baby-blue gown I'm made
to wear hangs over me
like a parachute, but it's open
in the front so I still feel
naked and exposed.

EXAM

When Dr. Greene examines me,
her ebony hands are icicles
against the hot magma of my skin.

She presses her fingertips into

my joints and asks if it hurts
here   here   or here.

Her palms feel like sandpaper
scrubbing against my skin.
I   WiNcE.

Dr. Greene: *On a scale of 1 to 10,*
                how much does it hurt?

She shows me a chart with smiley
faces that get sadder and sadder
the higher the number.

I point to the number 8.

She tells me to lift my chin
and look UP.

The yellow lights blink around
my eyes and make the ceiling spin.

She uses her peace fingers
to massage circles under my chin,
she checks for swelling.

If only she knew that all of me
feels SwOlLeN—an inflated
balloon ready to   P   O   P!

I SiGh.

She opens my gown a little more.
She presses the stethoscope against my spine.

She listens to the thump
                    ThUmP
                              tHuMp
of my swimming heart.

DR. GREENE ASKS ME QUESTIONS

Dr. Greene: *Can you stretch like this?*

Me: *Yes, but it hurts.*

Dr. Greene: *Can you bend like this?*

Me: *No, it hurts.*

Dr. Greene: *Are you stiff in the mornings?*

Me: *Sometimes I feel like the Tin Man.*

Dr. Greene: *How long has this been going on?*

Me: *A couple months maybe?*

MAMI WANTS TO KNOW

The (?) curl that hangs
between Mami's brows
shakes side to side,
disappointed.

Mami wants to know:
*¿Por qué no me dijiste **antes***
de que te pusieras tan mal?

Why didn't I tell her **sooner**
about my statue-stiff
mornings and clumsy
collapses when I get
out of bed?

Why didn't I tell **her** sooner
that sometimes I limp
after I sit too long or
sleep in too late?

And now I really wish
Papi were here to help me
explain to Mami that
I didn't tell her about
how I was feeling
because the last time
I got sick with the flu
was after I had lied about
failing a test, and Mami
made me pray
              and pray
                        and pray.

She said I got sick
because my sins had not
been forgiven. She said liars
lie down with snakes
and no daughter of hers
would be a serpent.

SICK

Can a secret make
you sick? Is my secret the
s
u
n
k
e
n
ship, rotting me and
polluting me inside out?
Could Mami be right this time?

DR. GREENE ASKS TOO MANY QUESTIONS

Dr. Greene: *Is this the first time your joints have swelled?*

Me: *No . . . my knee has been swelling up . . .*

Dr. Greene: *And what does that feel like for you?*

Me: *It hurts like I hit my knee against a table. And it feels
hot when I touch it. And when I walk,
it feels like someone is grinding a rock
against my bones.*

Dr. Greene: *Does your knee swell often?*

Me: *Mostly in the mornings.
And sometimes after . . .*

Dr. Greene: *After what?*

Me: . . .

Dr. Greene: *Okay, can you tell me what an average*
day looks like for you?

Me: . . .

Dr. Greene: *What were you doing the day before*
these symptoms started?

Me: . . .

Dr. Greene: *Sometimes even the simplest things*
we don't think about can trigger symptoms
or illness. Like the foods we eat,
or the activities we partake in.

Me: . . .

Dr. Greene: *Anything, anything at all you could tell me*
would be helpful.

Me: . . .

SPEAK

Dr. Greene: *The more you can tell me*
about what you were doing before
you got sick, the more I can help you.

I try,
but I can't speak.

My mouth goes dry.
And the room feels small.

I can't say what I need
to say.

I know if Papi were here
he'd be able to speak for me.

Maybe he'd finally tell
Mami the truth.

And then I'd be able
to breathe again.

NO AIR

Dr. Greene cups my shoulder and
her pink lips stretch into a smile.

My heart skips and leaps
like "el mar debajo de la luna llena,"
as Madrina would say.

Mami: *Dile qué estabas haciendo. Dile.*

Mami wrings her hands like a sponge.
As if she's the one tossing and turning
the ship inside me round and round.

Dr. Greene: *The more I know, the more
I can help. You want to get better,
don't you?*

I nod.   I do.   I do.

I don't want to feel this way
anymore.

But I also don't want to hurt
Mami with the truth.

Dr. Greene: *If you want me to help you,*
you have to talk to me.

I count my toes and watch
as the salt water I carry inside me
rains down on the checkered floor.

I inhale and exhale deeply,
and I know there is only one
way out of this storm.

Me: *I was at a swim meet the day before.*

Mami gasps and sucks all the air
right out of the room and right
out of my lungs.

I am learning it is possible
to drown without water.

TRAPPED

My secret is a shark
circling around us.

Dr. Greene hands me a tissue.
Mami paces the room.

Dr. Greene: *Honey, why are you crying?*
I know it's hard to be sick
like this for so long, but we're going to
find out what's wrong with you.
It's good that you're an active girl.
Swimming is good for you.

Mami huffs.

I nod and try to find more
words to speak and explain
myself to Mami and to the
doctor, but I don't
think I have any left.

They were swallowed up by
Mami's gasp,
Mami's disapproving eyes,
Mami's (?) curl shaking,

no
no
no.

RUN

Dr. Greene says:

I want to run
some tests and when the results
come back, I will give you a call.

For now, I am going to prescribe
some antibiotics.

Keep taking over-the-counter
medications to lower the fever
and help with the pain.

Mami, trying to be friendly
and keep her composure, quivers
her lips into a small smile.

She takes the prescription
in her trembling hands.

I hop off the exam table,
get dressed, and walk slowly
out of the room with Mami.

When the door closes behind us,
it swishes like the soft
ocean song I miss:
Make a wish
             wish
                    wish.

And so I squeeze my eyes
shut, rub the Larimar stone
in my pocket, and wish
my legs were strong enough
to   *RUN*   out of here
     RUN   away from Mami
RUN   into the arms
of the ocean and
be held.

PAPI CALLS

I don't know what he
says to Mami, but all she
says is: *Don't bother,*
the appointment is over.
Then she shuts her mouth like a door.

AN AWFUL SILENCE

Even during the blood draw,
when a small woman with small hands
squeezes my forearm and sticks me
with a needle to fill one, two, three, four,
five vials of blood—

Even as I limp to the parking lot
and Mami loops her arm
around mine so I can lean into
her and walk with a little less
ache in my legs—

Even in the car as she turns on
the radio and a song about forgiveness
and redemption plays on the Spanish
Christian radio station—

Even when someone honks at us
as we wait under a red light
and watch a tourist drop
an empty Doritos bag in the street without
looking back—

Even as we pull into the driveway
and the engine sputters off,
and the radio fades out and I sigh
the sigh of a thousand sorrows,
and reach out and say—

I'm sorry.

Even after all that—

Mami says nothing.

And I'm beginning to wonder
if maybe from now on,
it's better if I say nothing too.

MOTHERING MY WOUNDS

The doctor's visit
wore me out
like an old shoe.

Back in bed,
I rub my aching
wrists and nurse
my wounds.

The ones I can see
and the ones
I can't.

The ones that ache,
burn, and eat me up
from the inside out.

Maybe they are all
the same wound
and I just didn't know it
until today.

THE SOUND OF ANGER

Downstairs, Mami and Papi are FiGhTiNG.
Mami cooks and ScReAmS while Papi (and I) listens.

Canned goods SmAcK against countertops.
The fridge opens and sLaMs shut.

Wooden spoons TaP! tAp! TAP! against pots and pans.
Mami's questions HuRL out of her like cannonballs.

BETRAYED

Mami: *How could you LET her?*
Why would you keep a secret like this from me?
How LONG has this been going on?

> **Papi:** *Patty, cálmate! It's just swimming!*
> *In a POOL!*
> *It's not even in the big, wide, SCAAARY ocean.*
> *For God's —*

Mami: *DON'T use the Lord's name in vain!*
I don't care WHERE she's swimming.
I don't like it. It's not SAFE!
And you LIED to me FOR MONTHS!

> **Papi:** *¡Ay Dios mío!*
> *They have lifeguards and I am there watching*
> *over her EVERY minute. And I only lied*
> *because I knew if I told you, you'd react like this!*

Mami: *You know how I feel about water.*
YOU know! And yet you BETRAYED me!
You BOTH did. And YOU put her in harm's way.

            Papi: *She loves the water. It makes her HAPPY.*
                         Ani DESERVES to be happy.

The gas stove ClIcK, cLiCk, CLICKS on.
Mami slaps a spatula down on the counter.

Mami: *I don't care if she loves the water,*
and I don't care if she hates me for this,
but there will be
    NO more daddy-daughter dates,
        NO more swimming,
            NO more swim team or swim meets.

WHY

Why does it feel like
telling the truth is worse
than keeping a secret
or telling a lie?

Why does it feel like
everyone else can decide
what to do with my body
except for me?

Why is this happening
to me?
Why me?
    WHY me?
        Why ME?

TEXTING

Me: *Mami found out about the swim meet*
and swim practice.

Maria Tere: *How?*

Me: *I had to tell her.*
The doctor said the only way
   I would get better was if she knew
EVERYTHING.
   I wanted to get better so I can
be strong enough to swim again.
   But now I'll probably never be allowed
near the water as long as I live.

Maria Tere: *Oh no. What happened?*

Me: *Mami said no more swimming.*
   No more swim team.

Maria Tere: *I'm sorry. Are you ok?*

Me: *No.*

I put the phone down
too tired to keep texting
and wonder if I'll ever be "ok"
because there's a bonfire burning
me up inside and Mami's taken away
the only water that will help put it out.

HOW I'M FEELING

Papi sings:
Ani aguas . . . Ani aaaa-guaaas

He knocks on my door
and pushes it open.
It creaks and moans
like an old woman
with old bones who's had
to live through too many
storms.

Papi shimmies into
my room before
I've even had a chance
to say come in or go away.

Papi: *How are you feeling, mi reina?*

Me: *Angry. Where were you today?*

Papi: *I got stuck at work. I'm sorry.*
     Please forgive me. I was on
my way, pero Mami told me
     to come home. I wanted to be there.
I should have been there. I'm sorry.

I'm too tired to be angry,
so I fall into Papi's arms
and soak his uniform
with my too-tired-to-be-angry
tears.

HOW I'M REALLY FEELING

Papi: *¿Mi reina, qué te pasa?*

Me: *I am tired*
            sad
                scared.

I use these words but they
are not how I really feel.

I don't know the words
for this alone-ness
that makes me feel
like a single speck of a star
in the middle of a dark sky
no one is looking up at.

I don't know the words
for this frustration
with my own body
and what I want it to do
but can't.

I don't know if there is
a word for the fear
that I have of never being
myself again.

PAPI'S PROMISE

Papi: *Everything you're feeling is normal.*
We'll get through this one day at a time.

Me: *What about swimming?*

Papi's shoulders sag
like a worn-out rag doll.
His eyes go dark
like a midnight river.
He sighs and pulls me
in for a hug.

I breathe in his peppermint
skin and wait for him
to tell me what I already
know he's going to say.

Papi: *Mami doesn't think*
swimming is a good idea right now.
And neither do I.

I pull away from him,
shocked that he agrees with Mami.
He pulls me back in.

Papi: *Just for NOW.*
Until you can get better.
That's what's important now.

Me: *AM I going to get better, Papi?*

Papi: *Yes. You are.*

SOUP & SORRIES

Later, Mami enters my room
with a steamy bowl of sancocho.

Garlic, onion, cilantro, and other spices
my nose cannot name scent the air.

I sit up.

Mami circles around my bed
and sets the bowl on my nightstand.

She places the back of her hand
on my forehead to check my temperature.

My fever broke some time ago.

Her knuckles glisten with sweat
from my face.

She sighs one big breath and the thick
air between us hardens like frozen honey.

Me: *Mami, I really am sorry I—*

She lifts a spoonful of sancocho to my mouth
and then pat, pat, pats my knee.

Her dark eyes CuT into me.

Mami's voice is a w a v e that bends
but doesn't break.

Mami: *No more lies.*
　　　　No more secrets.
　　　　　　No more swim team.

Mami pats my knee one more time as if
laying down the final brick to a house

I will never live in.

HONOR THY MOTHER

Mami: *La Biblia says "Honor thy father*
   AND thy mother."
         But you did not do that.
   You and your father kept
         secrets from me
   AND you told your madrina things
         you didn't tell me. I am your mother
   AND you did not honor me.
         Perhaps that is why you are
   now so sick.

I blink back tears and realize
that Mami and I are two islands drifting
farther
         and
                  farther
                           apart.

CATEGORY 2: (SEA) SICK

July

QUESTIONS

When I don't come
to practice for a couple
of weeks, Paola
and Pilar text me
a lot of questions:

Where are you?
      What's wrong?
Why aren't you at practice?
      Are you coming to the swim meet?
Coach says you're sick, is it true?
      We miss you.
When are you coming back?

And because I don't
know the answers to
some of their questions,

and because I don't
want to disappoint them
with the truth,

I delete
their messages
and I don't answer
any of their questions.

FOURTH OF JULY

On the Fourth of July
I am stuck at home
with my family, feeling
unwell and lonely because
I'm used to spending this day
with my friends.

I know Maria Tere is out
near the seawall
or down on the Strand
dancing to the music
of the marching bands
at the parade
or getting ready to watch
the fireworks
on Pleasure Pier.

She's been sending me
pictures and updates,
but it's not the same.

I haven't missed an
Independence Day Parade
along the seawall
my whole life!

We only live two blocks
from where the parade
passes through and
listening to it outside
my window
makes this all worse.

OUTSIDE MY WINDOW

I can hear
the bass drum pounding
and the trumpets
and trombones screeching
and groaning
in the distance.

I can hear
people cheering and
singing along to the music
blaring from the colorful
floats.

I can hear
tiny bang snaps
CrAcK, CrAcK, CrAcKLing
and PoP, pOp, POPPING
in the street.

After a series of very loud
pops and cracks, Matti rushes
into my room and JuMpS
Up and DoWn on my bed
and giggles.

The mattress bounces
and its springs poke and press
against my skin.
It feels prickly and painful
but not enough for me
to ask him to stop.

Matti squeals.
I toss a pillow at him
and when he tries to catch it,
he falls and I blow raspberries
on his tummy and
he laughs
     and laughs
              and laughs.

I am grateful
that this is one of the few
things about my life
that hasn't changed.

A NICE SURPRISE

Right before the fireworks
are scheduled to start
I hear a tiny knock, knock,
knock on my bedroom door.

When I look
it's Maria Tere holding
two cups of Dippin' Dots
ice cream!

Maria Tere: *I couldn't let you watch
the fireworks by yourself.*

I get up as quickly as
my body will allow
and I give her a big hug.

Matti hops up behind me
and whines,

What about me?
Can I get some ice cream?

Me: *Of course, I'll share*
mine with you.

Maria Tere: *I will too.*

She helps me downstairs
and takes me to one of
the rocking chairs on the porch.
She sits in the other chair,
sets Matti on her lap,
and we eat our ice cream
in silence until the fireworks
begin and Matti shrieks
and covers his ears.

We laugh and eat and rock
and watch the fireworks
together and for a moment
I feel a little less
alone.

NO RELIEF

The tests Dr. Greene ran are "inconclusive."
She says I'm not infectious
but I do have a lot of inflammation.

She gives me some medicine
to reduce the swelling, and the fevers
have mostly stopped, but I still don't
feel like myself.

It has been weeks and weeks
of pulsing pain in my elbows and knees.
Red rashes on my hips and stomach.
In the morning I'm still sticky slow-moving
m o l a s s e s.

I am more tired than I have ever been.

No matter how much I sleep or rest,
rest or sleep, I am an ocean of lava
and all I can do is lie down and try
not to burn.

CLEAN UP, CLEAN UP, EVERYBODY DO YOUR SHARE

To deal with what she
    does not understand,
Mami cleans
    and cleans,
        and cleans,
            and is never done.
Clean up the bathroom.
    Clean up the halls.
        Clean up, clean up all
the mess,
    the dirt,
        the prints
            on the finger-smudged door.
Clean up, clean up,
    the clothes and shoes
        scattered on the floor.
WiPe.
    DuSt.
      MoP.
        S w E E p.
One more time,
    sCrUb,
        wAx,
            wAsH,
                rInSe.
Repeat.
    Do it all again,
        and again.

TOGETHER

After a couple of weeks
on the new medication,
I am less swollen
and have more energy.

Mami notices:
¿Ya te sientes mejor?

Me: *Yes, I feel better.*

Mami smiles, then rubs
the back of my head and
kisses the heart-shaped mole
on my temple.

Mami: *How about we clean
your room now and change the sheets?*

I agree because
Mami is being nice
and I want this to last.

When we clean together,
it feels better than when
Mami cleans alone.
Because when we clean
together, she hums along
to the religious songs
on the radio.

When we clean together,
she sways her hips instead
of stomping her feet.

BY THE GRACE OF GOD

While we clean, she digs
through my pants pockets and
finds the stones Madrina
gave me.

She grips them tight
in her hand and says:

No more stones, okay?
You will get better
by the grace of God.

She throws the stones in
the trash.

LIES & LARIMAR

When Mami is not
looking I dig the Larimar
stone out of the trash
and shove it in my gym bag
hoping it will one day help
me say everything I want to say.

FRIENDSHIP

Even though the medicine
is helping me some,
I still have bad days.
I never really know what
I am going to feel like
from one day to the next.

So, when I'm bored
and stuck at home all day,
one muggy afternoon in
mid-July,
I ask if Maria Tere can skip
her summer camp and come
over to hang out with me
and Madrina says yes.

Mami and Madrina are never
mad at each other for long.
Mami forgave Madrina
for not telling her about
my aches and pains after
Madrina came over
with empanadas and helped
Mami put up new curtains.
Mami has always said
their friendship is stronger
than any fight.

After Madrina drops
Maria Tere off, Mami
leaves to get groceries and we
are left in charge of Matti.

While Matti builds and
destroys towers of blocks,
we talk about everything
I'm missing at the Y:

Maria Tere: *We're going to
the waterpark next week
on a field trip!*

*And oh! My coach had
her baby, it's a girl and she
named her Lacy.*

*Paola and Pilar keep asking
about you. But I haven't told
them you might not be coming back.*

She complains about the sweaty
locker room smell I'm
actually beginning to miss,
because anything is better
than being cooped up in
this house week after week.

GIRLFRIENDS & GRILLED CHEESES

When we get hungry
and Mami isn't home yet,
we all chow down
on Takis and grilled cheese
sandwiches.

We play cards
on my bed, but

only Go Fish because
it's the only game Matti
knows how to play.

Maria Tere shuffles
the deck because my fingers
curl and I can't flip or fold
the stack. We let Matti win
and he brags about being
"the best."

We watch and re-watch
our favorite shows and
imagine when we'll meet
a man or woman
who will look at us like we're
made of starshine and magic.

When we're tired
and sleepy, Matti takes a nap
and Maria Tere curls up next to me,
squishes her feet against mine,
rests her head on my shoulder,
and asks me a question:

*Would you still be my friend
if I fell in love with a girl?*

Me: *Of course—as long as you don't
stop being my friend just 'cause
you got a girlfriend.*

Maria Tere: *Cross my heart and hope to die.
We are friends for life,
even when I get a girlfriend.*

HERMIT CRABS

Hurricane season started
in June and since then
Papi spends more and more
time at work,
more and more time
away.

He has to help train
the new rescue swimmers and make sure
he is ready for whatever
storms may come this season.

When he returns from
one of his short week-long
trips, he brings me
and Matti back some
seashells and a hermit crab.

Papi says:

I know it's not the same
    as being in the water,
but I brought you these
    reminders so you can feel
a little closer to the sea.

I stroke the seashells,
put the large one next to
my ear and listen to
the swish, swish, swish
of the waves.

Matti grabs a handful
of smaller shells and runs
upstairs, yelling:

I'm going to paint these
and put them with the rest
of my collection next to
Aquaman!

I place my hermit crab
in a clear case with sand
and rocks and watch it
poke its head in and out
of its shell.

Papi says:

I saw the hermit crab
       and thought of you because
hermit crabs can adapt
       to any shell they crawl
into and you are doing such
       a good job of adapting
to all of these changes too.

But when I look at
the hermit crab,
all I see is how it's able
to leave its hard shell
when it wants.

But I can never
leave my body,
my shell.

And I never thought
I'd be jealous
of something as simple
as a hermit crab.

TELL HIM

I don't tell Papi
how the hermit crab
makes me feel
because I don't want
to make him feel
bad.

Instead I say:

Thank you.
    I love it.

He hugs me and sighs
and I worry he will
start to cry.

But he doesn't.
Instead he says:

You know my job
    is to rescue people,
and right now, my number one
    mission is to rescue you
from this illness. And even
    though I know I'm gone

a lot, you have to know
      that I'm doing everything
I can to make sure
      you get better.

And even though I know
what he's saying is true,
I want to tell him
that I don't need him
to rescue me
or make me better—
that's what the doctors
are for.

I just need him to be HERE.

REPENT

Mami makes me go
    to church with her this week.

She believes I still need to repent
    for keeping secrets,
        for sinning against God.

The church is so cold,
    even the windows fog up
        with condensation.

The icy air that blows
    from the AC above the pews
        curls around my elbows and knees,
            and makes my joints seize up and ache.

I try to tell Mami that it hurts
    to be inside the church
        but she insists I stay seated.

She puts her hand on my forehead,
    checks for a temperature.

Mami: *You look fine. You're not*
                running a fever.

She shakes her head,
    her (?) curl of frustration
        bouncing up and down.

I'm learning that it's hard
    for people to understand things
        they can't see, or hear, or touch
            for themselves.

She guides me to the front pew.
　　She makes me kneel
　　　　　　for minutes and minutes
　　　　　　　　and minutes,

that feel like hours
　　and hours
　　　　and hours.

PENANCE

The wood grinds against
　　my kneecaps like glass
　　　　in a blender.

My hips PuLsE
　　like a red railroad
　　　　warning light.

I TwIsT and tUrN.
　　I grunt and stand up.
　　　　I can't focus on prayer
　　　　　　when my body bellows
　　　　　　　　in PaIn.

Mami points at the pew
　　and reminds me I'm here
　　　　to do my penance.

Mami: *Tienes que pedirle perdón al Señor.*
　　Solo él te salvara. Anda.
　　　　Cierra los ojos.
　　　　　　Get on your knees
　　　　　　　　and pray.

BARGAINING

I never pray
for forgiveness. Instead, I
close my eyes and beg God:
Change Mami's heart so I can
swim and be myself again.

AQUAMAN & ME

Later that night after church,
Matti comes to my room and
curls up under the covers next to me.

His brown curls frizz and wisp
against my skin and tickle my chin.
He shoves his Aquaman action
figure in my face.

Matti: *Here, take this.*

Me: *Why are you giving this to me?*

Matti: *It's Aquaman. You can **borrow** him.*

Me: *Okay. Why?*

He rolls his owl-brown eyes at me
as if I had asked the dumbest
question in the world.

Matti: *Beccauuusssee . . . didn't you say
you were a dolphin?*

Me: *You have a good memory. I did say that.*

Matti: *Well, Aquaman can talk
to sea creatures. Maaayybeee,
    he can talk to you and it will make you feel better.*

He buries his head under my arm.
My body becomes a shell
I promise to use to protect him.

ANOTHER VISIT WITH DR. GREENE

Dr. Greene: *On a scale of 1 to 10*
how much does your body hurt today?

I point to the sad smiley face
under the number 6.

Dr. Greene's Pepto-Bismol–pink
lips purse into a worried half smile.

Dr. Greene*: I'm concerned that your*
symptoms aren't improving.

On my left Mami sighs and wrings
her hands with worry.

On my right Papi gently squeezes my knee
and taps his foot on the floor, frustrated.

He believes it is his job to "make me better,"
and because I am not better, it makes him angry.

I sit between them, pain shooting
up and down my leg like a dozen tiny

jellyfish tentacles RiPPiNg my nerve
endings to pieces.

Dr. Greene: *I'm going to refer you*
to a specialist.

She scribbles on a crisp notepad.
She checks off boxes and signs her name
at the bottom.

BETWEEN A ROCK AND A HARD PLACE

Papi: *What does she need a specialist for?*
 Why can't you tell us what's wrong with her?
  Is it serious?
   Will she be okay?

Papi's voice gets heavy like one
of his leather combat boots
and the questions stomp,
   StOmP
    sToMp
out of him.

Dr. Greene shuffles her papers
and clears her throat.

Dr. Greene: *My expertise in this area is limited.*
It's best if she sees a specialist who can
 properly diagnose her and get her
  the treatment she needs.

Papi: *What kind of doctor is this specialist?*

Dr. Greene: *Dr. Simpson is a neurologist.*
He specializes in diagnosing and treating
 ailments of the brain and spinal cord.
  He will likely want to run more tests
   to find out what's going on.

Papi: *What KIND of tests?*

Papi wants to be in command,
but he sounds like he's losing
control.

Dr. Greene: *Well, he'll probably have more*
blood drawn. Possibly a CT scan or an MRI
     of her brain. This will help us determine
          if the cause of the fever and swelling
             is because something is affecting
         her brain and central nervous system
     or if it is something else entirely.

Papi stares down at the referral
the doctor has handed him.

Mami turns and turns her wedding
ring around her finger as if the answer
to all of my problems could be found there.

I rub the Larimar stone in my pocket,
look back and forth between
Mami,   Papi,   and Dr. Greene,
hoping someone will ask ME
what I want and how I feel.

BUTTERFLIES, BRAINS & THE BOTTOM OF THIS

Dr Greene's hazel eyes flutter
like butterfly wings in spring
as she says:

Don't you worry about a thing.
Dr. Simpson is a very good
neurologist. All he's going to do
is take a look at your brain.
We want to rule
some things out before making

154

an official diagnosis.
And we can't know anything
for sure until we run
some more tests.
But we're going to get
to the bottom of this.
Okay?

STONE SILENT

I want to tell her
that my head doesn't hurt.
That I don't think
the sickness is inside
my brain.

I want to tell her
it's in my bones
and in the rest
of my burning
body.

I want to tell Mami
and Papi
that I'm scared and sad
and tired of not being
able to do what
I want to do.

My sweaty hands
slip over the Larimar
stone in my pocket,
but as I open my mouth

to speak,
my throat clumps
like a fistful of wet
sand.

Even Larimar
can't help me say
what I want to say.

NO PEACE

Dinner that night is quiet
except for Matti, who wants to tell us
what he did at Madrina's house
all afternoon while we were
at the doctor.

He bounces up and down
in his chair while he describes
every last detail.

Matti: *We painted seashells,*
then we painted rocks,
and then she let me watch
Spider-Man: Into the SPIDER-VERSE*!*
And did you know
that Spider-Man looks like ME!
Not like the other *Spider-Man.*
And then me and Maria Tere
played basketball but
I only made one basket
because—

Mami slams her fork
down on the table:

Ay Matti! ¡YA! Please
let us eat in peace.

Matti sulks in his seat
for a moment, then pushes
his plate away and runs
off to watch TV.

That's when Papi gets up
from the table and says:

We need milk. Come with me,
Ani, let's go for a drive.

PAPI'S GOD

We don't really need milk.
I saw we still had half
a gallon in the fridge
this morning.

But I think Papi wants
to get out of the house.
And I'm glad because
I wanted to get out too.

Since the doctor's appointment,
it's felt like I can't catch
my breath.

Even though there's a corner
store nearby, Papi decides
to go to the big grocery store
on the seawall.

He opens the windows
and lets the seaside air
flow through the car.

At a stoplight Papi closes
his eyes. I close mine too.
We take a deep breath
together.

Papi: *The water makes*
everything better. Doesn't it?

Even though I wish I could
be IN the water, Papi is right.
Just being near it is enough right
now. Just being near it almost
makes me forget about
my pain and the doctors
and the tests.

The light turns green and
I ask Papi a question:

Papi, do you believe in God?

Papi: *You know I do. Why?*

Me: *Because you rarely go to church with us.*

Papi: *I don't think you have to go to*
church to believe in God.
    I believe God is everywhere.
        God is in the air,
            and the flowers,
      in the trees,
    and in the breeze.
My God is also right here . . .

He points to the center
of his chest where his mint-
green guayabera rises and falls.

I look back out to the seawall
where the waves rush in and
slip back
          rush in
and slip back.

Me: *If that's true, Papi, then MY God*
is in the ocean and the sea.

Papi wraps his arm around me,
and kisses my forehead.

Papi: *I think you're right.*

ONE MORE QUESTION

Me: *Papi, do you think God is fair?*

Papi: *I think God does what he . . . or*
she thinks is best.

Me: *If that's true, then why is God*
doing this to me?

Papi: *I think God wants us to be*
the best version of ourselves.
        Maybe in ways that we can't
                really understand yet. All of this
        is going to help you become
who you're meant to be.

THE LAST MEET

Papi at home and
Maria Tere on the phone
remind me that this
Saturday is the final
swim meet of the season.

Papi at home and
Maria Tere on the phone
ask me if I want to go
to cheer on Paola and Pilar.
They ask me if I want
to get out of the house.

I tell Papi and
Maria Tere:

No.
No.
No.

And they keep asking:

Why?
Why?
Why?

And all I can say is:

Because I'm in too much pain.

ON A SCALE OF 1 TO 10

How much does it hurt
my heart that I cannot
watch or be a part of
the last meet of season?

10!

    10!

10!

INSOMNIA

Most
nights I
cannot sleep.
The streetlights
outside my window blink
and flicker yellow. The sea salt
air settles in my room, on the walls
and in my sheets. All I want to do is
JUMP into the ocean and swim my aches and
pains away. But the sea and sand and
swimming feel as distant as a lone
kite flapping in the sky.
Something I can see,
but cannot
reach out
and
grab.

AND, AND, AND

The next week
after more tests and
an MRI and
a CT scan and
more poking and
prodding and
temperature checks and
blood draws and
step on this, and
lie on that and
move like this and
bend like that and
does this hurt and
on a scale of 1 to 10 and
when did it start and
does it tingle and
how often does it ache and
does it shoot or throb and
does it pulse or burn and
and
and
and
and
and
after all of that—
the neurologist's results
came back:

Inconclusive.

SLUSHIES AT MURDOCH'S

It is Saturday, and so far
today has been one of my
"good days," so Mami
invites Madrina and Maria Tere
over for dinner.

After we eat, Maria Tere
and I decide to go
to Murdoch's.

Matti asks if he can come
too but we say no.
We want girl time—alone.
But we promise to bring
him back some candy.

We walk the four blocks
up to Murdoch's on the seawall
for slushies and people watching.

Murdoch's is a gift shop
like Madrina's, but it's
even more expensive and
made for the
beach-drunk tourists.

But it does have the best
slushies and snacks
in town.

It also has a breezeway
with a large deck that

faces the ocean and has
incredible views
of the sunset.

We grab our slushies:
blue raspberry for me,
cherry red for Maria Tere.

We walk out onto the deck
but there's nowhere to sit.
It's late July,
the peak of summer break,
and the island is crowded
with families and out-of-towners.
A few younger kids run
around us in circles and scream.
A couple leans against the
railing and kisses.
A country song plays on
the speakers and two women
sipping piña coladas sing along.

We stand around and wait
for a bit until an elderly couple
leaves and we snag the two
white rocking chairs
they were sitting in.

We look out over the deck.
The late afternoon air is
sticky and warm.
The sky swirls with
pink and purple.
The ocean shimmers with
late afternoon sunlight.

Even with the hustle and
bustle of tourists, the island
feels calm tonight
and so do I.

SOON

Me: *The water is so beautiful.*
I wish I could jump in it
 and swim to the end of the Earth.

Maria Tere: *It is really nice today.*
You'll be back in the water soon,
 you'll see. You're gonna get better.

Me: *Am I?*

I bite my lip to stop the waterfall
of tears that has been building
behind my eyes for weeks.

Maria Tere's voice cracks, fragile
like a fish bone snapped in half.

Maria Tere: *Yes!*

Me: *When? I just saw ANOTHER specialist.*

Maria Tere: *You mean aside from the brain doctor?*

Me: *Yes, the brain doctor sent me to a specialist in Houston.*
And that doctor took more blood and ran more tests.

And they still haven't told me what's wrong.
How can I get better if they don't even know what's wrong?

Maria Tere: *I'm sorry they don't know.*
But just be patient, okay? I'm sure they'll figure it out
soon.

She holds my hand and we watch
the seagulls slide and glide
through the air.

Soon, soon, soon, I repeat,
in rhythm with the waves
lapping along the shore,
hoping but not knowing
if it's true.

MY HEART

When we get back to my house
Madrina and Mami are on the porch
sipping agua de Jamaica.

Maria Tere runs inside to use
the bathroom and Mami follows after
her to pack up leftovers for Maria Tere
and Madrina to take home.

Madrina and me sit on the steps
of the porch in silence until
she turns to look at me. She places
her hand on my chest and whispers:

How are you, mi'ja?
      How is your heart?

And before I can stop myself, I tell her
about all the specialists, the inconclusive
test results and the painful pinpricks
when they take my blood.

I complain about Mami's cleaning sprees,
my insomnia and how her stones
haven't healed me or help me say what
I need to say.

Madrina doesn't say a word.
She just listens.

WE BREATHE

When I'm all out of breath
with nothing left to say,
Madrina pulls a small
bottle out of her pocket.

She sprinkles a few drops
of lavender oil into her palms,
massages it on my neck and
shoulders. I melt into Madrina's
arms and I let her hold me.

When she inhales,
    I inhale.
When she exhales,
    I exhale.

Madrina: *Mi amor, remember*
the stones are meant to support you
        on your healing journey.
                They are not meant to solve
        or save you from your problems.
It is not your fault you are still sick.
        Our bodies are complex and sometimes
                there is no quick or easy remedy.
        These things take time. Now repeat after me:
I am safe.

Me: *I am safe.*

I am strong.

Me*: I am strong.*

I let go.

Me: *I let go.*

Sometimes the only thing we have control over is our breath. So, let go, mi amor, and just breathe.

FISHERS OF MEN

The next morning, Papi
shakes and wakes me and
Matti up with the Sunday
sunrise and tells us to
get dressed.

Papi: *¡Vamos a pescar!*

He whistles and sings
a bold bolero I remember
from when we visited
Quisqueya
a few years ago.

I try to tell him that
even though I was fine
yesterday, today
my knees ache and my
hips hurt, but he insists.

Papi: *Fishing on the pier is easy.*
Fishing is calm. Fishing will help
you forget all your problems.

I do not tell him that sitting
or standing too long on the pier
will make me hurt more.

I do not tell him because
Papi has not been this
excited about anything
in a while.

Matti is sleepy and I am
in pain, so we grumble
and groan our way through
breakfast waffles
and brushing our teeth.

We pack the rods, the bait,
the hooks, the chairs, and
the cooler in the truck.

I wrap my right knee and
make sure to pack my pain
medication just in case.

We hug and kiss Mami goodbye
and she asks us to be careful.

Mami has never really worried
about us fishing on the pier
because she knows we won't
be getting in the water.

And also Mami REALLY
loves eating fresh fish, so she
sends us on our way without
a fuss.

Once in the car, Papi opens
the windows and lets the breeze
blow in.

The air smells and tastes like fish.
A fog rolls and floats over
the city streets like a ghost
in a wedding dress.

Papi drives as if he has
everywhere
and nowhere to go.

FISH BALLET

We unload the bed
of the truck.

Papi bathes us in bug
spray and sunscreen.

Matti sNeEzEs and squints
his still sleepy eyes.

The sun slips through
a cotton of clouds and
reflects on the water
like diamonds in a
black bowl.

Beneath the pier, the fish
scurry and swim
in a synchronized ballet
I could watch all day.

Papi prepares the line
and hands each of us
a rod.

He flings his into the water.

I lower mine gently over
the wooden railing as if
the water were made of
glass I do not want to break.

We wait
         and wait
                  and w a i t.

FISH FOOD

Papi,
why are
we here? Matti
moans from
heat exhaustion. He wipes
his forehead with his sleeve. Papi takes off   his
hat and fans himself and Matti with it. Then, like a   preacher
giving a sermon, he deepens his voice and says: *Give a man*   *a fish and*
ll eat for a day. Teach him how to fish and he'll have food for the rest of his life. Matti
ɔmps his foot. *But I'm not even a man yet!* I giggle. Matti has a point. Papi
ɔreathes in the morning mist and chuckles. *What I'm saying is,*   *I want to*
prepare you for when I'm not here. I want to prepare you for   *whatever*
life may bring your way, whatever life path you may choose.   *This—*
he jiggles his fishing   rod
a little—*is for your*
own good.

177

PATIENCE

We wait some more.

Seagulls sweep and sail
over the water.
They claw at and compete
with us for any dancing
fish that dare to
J u M p
out of the water.

I adjust and readjust
myself in my chair
because my body burns
for movement.

I don't know how much
longer I can sit still
before all my joints will
swell and buckle beneath
the weight of waiting.

Me: *Papi, when can we leave?*
We're not catching anything.

Papi sees my pained face
and sets his rod down
on the banister of the bridge.

He places his palm
on my forehead to check
my temperature.

When will Mami and Papi
realize that my illness
is about more than just
my temperature?

Papi: *You're warm, but that's*
probably just the sun.
You look fine. Let's just wait
a little longer. Remember, all good
things come to those who wait.

GOOD AGAIN

While we wait
for the fish to bite
and for our lines to twist
and turn with trout, red-snapper
or flounder,
all I can wonder is—

How long will I have to
w a i t
before my life
gets *good* again?

A DIAGNOSIS

Finally,
there is a doctor who knows
what's wrong with me.

Tuesday, while Papi
is at work, Dr. Castro,
the specialist from Houston,
calls the house and
speaks to Mami.

I can hear the doctor
on the other line.
Her voice is thin and
hisses like a balloon deflating
in midair.

Dr. Castro: *Based on her labs,*
her recent medical history,
*   and because her symptoms have*
persisted for more than six weeks,
*   I think your daughter has*

Juvenile
        Idiopathic
                Arthritis

We should schedule an appointment
*   to discuss her treatment options.*

Mami walks to another
room and I cannot hear
the rest of their conversation.

TSUNAMI

JuVeNiLe
iDiOpAtHiC
ArThRiTiS

My legs begin to tremble
as if each word
were an earthquake
shaking and breaking
beneath the sea of me.

I

Later that night,
when Mami and Papi
think I've gone to sleep,
they whisper in the living
room about

What's next? And
    What do we do? And . . .
What is this? And . . .
    Why Ani?   *And . . .*
How did this happen? And . . .
    What treatment options? And . . .
Let's look it up. And . . .

because our house carries
sound
I hear words like

Idiopathic . . .   *Idiopático . . .*
    Inflammation . . .   *Inflamación . . .*
Incurable . . .   *Incurable . . .*

And whether they say
the words in English
or in Spanish, I know
they are talking about me.

So why am

I

not a part
of the conversation?

DRIVE

On Friday, we have to
drive to Houston to meet
with the specialist.

After we drop Matti off
at Madrina's and start
the drive out of town, I clear
my throat, take a deep breath
and I let my questions flood
our car like the ocean floods
our island during a storm:

What did the doctor say
    about my diagnosis?
What is Juvenile Idiopathic Arthritis?
    What does idiopathic *even mean?*
What's the treatment?
    How long will I feel like this?

Papi adjusts his seat belt
and chuckles, his eyes darting
back forth between Mami and me
in the rearview mirror.

Papi: *Okay, one thing at a time.*
According to Dr. Castro, you have some kind of arthritis
that children can get. Idiopathic *means they don't know where*
it comes from and—

Mami shoots Papi an icy stare.

Mami: . . . *AND, we're not going
to jump to any conclusions. We don't
    know all the details yet. Let's wait
and see what she tells us today.*

Papi looks at me through the
rearview mirror and tries to
crack a smile.
Mami sighs and shakes her
head. She tells Papi to keep
his eyes on the road and drive.

WAITING ROOM

Papi says
"good things come
to those who wait."

But nothing good
ever waits for me
on the other side

of the waiting
room door.

THIN

Dr. Castro,
the new specialist,
the one who diagnosed me,
is a rheumatologist.

She is a thin woman
with thin skin that moves
like r i p p l e s in the water.
Her thin black hair
wisps across her face
like tassels on a rope.
Her bronze skin and sing-
songy voice makes me
believe she is from an island.

Not like Galveston,
but an island like Mami's
where the people speak
something other than English
and are not afraid
to sing and dance in the street.

Her office smells
like oranges and sunscreen
and the photographs
of children smiling, laughing
and playing in the sand,
on a trampoline,
and at the park remind me
of all the things I used to
be able to do.

IN A FISH NET

Mami slumps and sighs,
the weight of it all
too much for her back
to bear.

Papi shuffles the green
and pink pamphlets in his
hands. He flips through
them without reading
a single word, rolls
them up and
    tAp,
           TaP,
                    TAPS
them against his knee.

Dr. Castro crosses
her legs and leans
back in her café
con leche leather chair.

She begins to explain
my diagnosis, but the
space between my ears
fills with water.

Her words swim and
swirl in my mind
like a school of fish
swimming away
from a fish net.

I reach for a word   here
or   there
but am only able to
CaTcH a phrase,
a gesture, a sigh

. . . *common misconception . . . under the age of sixteen . . .*
. . . *medications . . . treatment . . . physical therapy . . .*
. . . *a rare disease . . . outgrow . . .*
. . . *reduce swelling . . . a normal life . . .*

DIS-EASE

The words Dr. Castro
uses to describe
Juvenile
        Idiopathic
                Arthritis
are hard to say
and some even
harder to spell:

autoimmune
antibodies
chronic
inflammation
musculoskeletal
rheumatic
systemic
disease

The only word I do know
the meaning of—

The only word I cannot
un-hear—

The only word that KnOcKs
against my ears
like a stranger   PoUnDiNG
on a door begging
to be let in is

DISEASE!
    dis-EASE!
        DIS-ease!

TEARS

When Dr. Castro is done
talking,
tears trickle
d
o
w
n
my face
and into my mouth.

My tears
the only salt water
I get to taste
these days.

METAL AGAINST PETALS

Dr. Castro hands me
and Mami tissues,
because she's crying
too.

The doctor's brown eyes thin,
and squint, circle and peer
over the thin blue frames
of her glasses and
I think she may also
begin to cry.

But she doesn't.

Instead, Dr. Castro gets up
and kneels next to me.
The gold metal name tag
pinned to her white
lab coat press against
my shoulder.

Her spaghetti fingers
pull my hand
into hers and she
squeezes it
as if it were
a delicate rose
whose petals
will crumble
at the slightest touch.

BRAVE

Dr. Castro: *You're a very brave girl.*
I know you're going to get through this.
   Okay?
You're going to be okay.
   Just hang in there.
Be brave. Okay?

Okay.
   Okay?
      Okay!

               I think.
But what I really want
is to scream:
               I am NOT OKAY!

WEIGHT

A new ship anchors
inside my burning body.
I try to make it
float, but it is heavy. It plummets—
weighed down by sadness.

ON THE WAY TO THE CAR, I TEXT MARIA TERE ABOUT MY DIAGNOSIS

Maria Tere: *So does this mean you're gonna die?*

Me: *No! It's not a terminal illness.*

Maria Tere: *Is it contagious?*

Me: *No!*

Maria Tere: *Well, how did you get it?*

Me: *IDK.*
    The doctor says maybe
        the environment,
           maybe genetics.
      Maybe Mami was right
   and this is what I get for lying.

Maria Tere: *No! Don't you dare believe that.*

Me: *IDK what else to believe.*

Maria Tere: *Can they fix it? Is there a cure?*

Me: *No. No cure just treatments.*

Maria Tere: *Oh . . . I'm so sorry amiga.*

Me: *Me too.*

MAMI MOURNS & PAPI PRETENDS

Before Papi starts the car
Mami makes us pray.
Papi lays his hands
on top of mine.
We bow our heads
obedient and we wait
for Mami's words.

But they do not come.

Mami: *Ay mi niña,*
    ay mi niña.

Is all she can mutter
and mourn between
sobs and suspiros
that sound like a summer storm.

Unsure of what to do
Papi begins to pray.
Papi pretends everything
is going to be okay.

Papi: *Senor Dios, we ask that you take care of Ani...*
We ask for strength as a family to bear this burden together...
We ask for the bravery to face whatever may come next.
In Jesus' name we pray. Amen.

BUT I DON'T WANT TO BE

brave
I just want to be
ME
again.

CATEGORY 3:
(TROPICAL) DEPRESSION

August

BURDEN

I am beginning to feel
like a burden.
Mami and Papi
shuttle me around
from one appointment
to the next and every day
there are forms
to fill out and
procedures and
pharmacy calls and
questions to ask and
"please call back," and
results and receipts and
bills and pills and
sometimes I hear Mami
crying in the bathroom and
sometimes Papi says he's
going for a long drive and
he doesn't come back
for hours and
some days Mami and Papi
fight about the bills and pills
and results and receipts
and pharmacy calls
and procedures and forms
and on and on it goes
waves of errands and chores
waves and waves of sadness
lapping endlessly along a shore.

HURT

I am not the only
one who is hurting from this
disease. Mami and Papi
must also mourn their active
carefree little girl who is now gone
for good.

BECAUSE I AM SICK

The doctor prescribes:

1. Pain pills—for the pain
2. Steroids—to suppress my immune system
3. Anti-inflammatories—for fevers and inflammation
4. Physical therapy—for my joints

A HARD PILL TO SWALLOW

The pain pills are supposed to treat and tame the fire in me. I gulp them down with a glass of water every morning and every night. They are thick and round and chalky white. They slip and slide down my throat. When I try to get up, the room spins and spins. They taste like rust and sit in my stomach like a spoiled root beer float. It's as if someone has clipped my fins. My skin swells red like an angry ocean tide. I limp and hobble, my disability something I cannot hide. Nausea bubbles in my belly. It feels like my mind is made of jelly. another difficult pill to swallow. Side effects swoop me up and spit me out. None of this is working! I just want to shout. My disability, a word that sounds so hollow. My body buckles, fumbles, and falls. I am a crumbling, poorly built seawall.

RANGE OF MOTION

My physical therapist,
Sophie, says my joints
are a clogged pipe
stuffed with sticky gum
and we need to work
to loosen up the gunk.

Twice a week, I stretch
and strengthen my body
into shapes and letters.

sQuAt   against the wall
ReAcH   toward the floor
ToUcH   my toes
StReTcH   my arms UP
and d o w n
into a Y then a T
BeNd and L U N G E
cUrL and L I F T

Sophie says:
Keep going. Keep trying.
You got this. This is going to help.

And so I
pLaNk and BrIdGe
    p u l l and RAISE
TwIsT and t u r n
    CrEaK and SpUtTeR.

FAITH & FAILURE

My body is an old
sink squeaking and
churning,
about to
        BURST!
But I can't seem to
        SPEAK
and tell Sophie
that I want to
        STOP!
Because it hurts
and tomorrow it will
hurt worse
before it feels better.

But she's the expert
and she knows
what she's doing,
at least I hope
that's true.

And so each
session becomes
an exercise in
faith and failure.

PLAYING PRETEND

After
physical therapy, I play
pretend with Matti. He holds Aquaman
with one hand and my old pink-and-purple My Little
Pony toys in the other. He tells me to build a tower with
magnetic tiles. He knocks the tower down and crowns himself
the king of the Magical Sea. When he gets bored playing inside,
we go outside and sit under the orange tree. We suck on orange
slices and make up stories. Today the sun is hot and the air is
humid. Matti digs a hole in the dirt and buries a seed. *Do you
think a new tree will grow here before you die?* he asks innocently.
I gasp, surprised. *What? Who said I'm going to die?* He pats the
soil down with a stick. *Mami says you're sick, which is why you
can't play tag like we used to. Don't sick people die?* I shake
my head and hug him close. *NO. Not all of them. I'm
not gonna die. I'll be here a long time to watch you
and that tree grow till it touches
the sky.*

LAST DAYS OF SUMMER BREAK

Most days I don't have much energy
to hang out or talk to anyone,
but on my really good days when
there is almost no swelling or pain,
Maria Tere comes over and we ride
our bikes up and down the street.

Most of the streets on this side of town
slope like a hill and because my legs still ache
even on my "good days," I walk my bike up the hill.

Even though Maria Tere can pedal fast and hard
she always walks her bike up the hill too.

Then, when I reach the top, I take in a breath,
hop on my bike, and let gravity
G   L   I   D   E   me down.

As we ride and glide we holler and howl.
When we reach the bottom, we giggle and pant.

Then we do it all over again.

Sometimes, when the breeze is really strong,
I spread my arms out like a bird and I imagine
that the wind blowing on my face and through
my hair is actually water and I am S W I M M I N G.

And for those few brief moments, I feel like
the old me and that makes me happy.

TAX-FREE WEEKEND

On tax-free weekend,
Mami takes me shopping
for shoes and school clothes.

Tax-free weekend
is the weekend
before school starts
and everything for school
like clothes, shoes
and school supplies are tax free.

Even though we know
the mall will be
crowded with customers,
Mami likes to shop
on tax-free weekend
because Mami
can never say no to
a good sale or discount.

When we arrive,
the mall is swarming
with other moms and
daughters doing
the same thing
we are about to do.

People pass and swish
by us carrying bags
and bags of clothes
and shoes and
stationery.

People rush and shove
and grab things.
They wait in long lines to pay.

At the department store,
I see girls my age
trying on dresses and jeans,
and shirts and pants.

They model their outfits
for their moms and friends.
They laugh and snap
selfies in the full-length mirror.

Once upon a time
that used to be me.

NO ENERGY

This morning I had
the energy
to get dressed and
come to the mall.
But now that we are
here,
I worry I won't have
the energy
or strength to get
through this day.

LIKE MOTHER LIKE DAUGHTER

When I step out
of the dressing room
in a yellow dress,
Mami smiles and says:

Wow, it's so pretty.

She strokes my hair
and tugs at the white collar
on the dress.

She smiles again.
*It's amazing how much
you look like me
when I was your age.*

She hands me another
item of clothing to try on.
I take it, but then I sit down
because I am tired.

I want this day to be fun.
I want to feel happy
like all the other girls
around me.

But my shoulders ache
from lifting and lowering
my arms to get in
and now out of this dress.
And I'm already out of breath.

Mami sees my reflection
in the mirror and it's
like she can read my mind.

She wraps her arm
around my shoulder
and squeezes a little too tight.

When I flinch, she apologizes:

I'm sorry.
You know what, we don't
have to try on any more.
I'll buy the ones you like
and we can try them on
at home. Where you can
go slow. We can just return
the ones that don't fit.
Why don't we get some lunch
and go home?

I smile and nod,
because Mami is being
nice and knows
just what to say.
And it makes me believe
that one day, things
between us might just be okay.

Maybe Mami
is finally beginning to
believe that my disease
includes more than what she
can ever touch or see.

AT THE FOOD COURT

Mami asks if I'm excited
about starting a new school year,
and because we have had a good day,
I feel like a tiny pebble
has been released from my
clogged-up throat
and the words come rushing
out and I am able to
tell her how I feel without
worrying how she'll react.

Me: *I want to go to school.*
I'm tired of being cooped up
at home, but . . . What if it
hurts too much to walk to
or sit in class? What if I get
too tired to focus? What if
they make fun of how I
have to limp sometimes? What if . . .

The tiny pebble creeps back
up and becomes a stone.
I know if I try to speak
again, the tears instead of words
will begin to flow.
Mami's eyes also water.
She holds my hand, sighs,
and then says the right thing again:

Mami: *What IF we just take*
it one day at a time?

REAL DADDY-DAUGHTER DATE

The next day, after
church with Mami,
Papi takes me on a real
daddy-daughter date.

I choose to wear
the yellow cotton dress
with pockets and a white collar
that Mami and me bought
at the mall the day before.

I show off my teal
toenails in a pair of cream-
colored sandals.
And I plant one of Mami's
marigolds in my hair.

Before we leave,
Papi packs us a picnic,
but won't tell me where
we're going.

He drives and drives
with the windows open.
The ocean air blows
through our curls.

Papi finds his favorite song
on his phone and turns
it up real loud.

A raspy old merengue
belts out from a man

and his guitar.
Papi TaP   tAP   TAPS
the steering wheel and hums.

Papi always plays his
favorite merengue
when he's happy.
And if Papi is happy,
I'm happy too.

FERRY RIDE

Papi puts the car in park.   fish and human food
   We watch the water   s w o o p i n g down for
      and point at the seagulls

When the captain says   as he walks
   it's safe to stand on deck,   W O B B L E
      Papi and the picnic basket

Hurry up, he says,
   forgetting that these days,   S l OoOoO w
      I still walk a little

We eat peanut butter   oranges
   and mango jelly sandwiches   and Takis and
      (Papi's only specialty)

Two Maltas   and melt in our mouths
   fizz and bubble   crumble in our hands
      on our tongues, while brownie bites

The ferry rocks us
        side to side.   its head above the water,
                A far-off dolphin peeks
then sinks back
        down into the
             sea.
The ocean waves
      SpLaSh and lap   a song that softens
           against the ferry—   the sadness inside me.

I miss the water,
        I say,
              and squint at the sun.   *I know,* Papi sighs.

His eyes are glossy
        with what I think Mami   would call nostalgia.
                and Madrina

Like he's wishing   ago.
          for something   from a long time

I miss the light
    that used to   *want her back.*
      shine from the ocean of your eyes.   *and I just*
               I miss my little girl,

I hold his hand   *Convince Mami.*
      and squeeze it tight.   *let me swim again.*
           If you want happy Ani back,

¿Como? How, Ani?
        Dime.
          I blink back tears and squeeze
                  his hand just a little harder.

Tell her the truth.

                       Tell her I'm a dolphin,   *is the water.*

                                       and my only home

PROMISES

Papi says he will
talk to Mami but he can't
promise she'll say yes.

SCARY & NEW

The night before school
starts, Matti comes to my room,
and he is crying:

I don't want to go to school.
It's too scary, and I'll be alone.

He's starting Pre-K
and he's been talking about
it for many weeks.
I know this is just
those first day jitters, because
I'm having them too.

Because I don't want
people to stare at my limp
or ask me questions
about my disease.
I want to feel accepted
and Matti does too.

I dry his tears and
give him my best pep talk:
Sometimes new things are
scary, but scary
doesn't have to mean it's bad,
it's just new, that's all.
You'll make lots of friends
and have so much fun. Just watch.

And I don't really know if
I'm saying these words for him
or me.

BACK TO SCHOOL

For the next two weeks,
I try to go to school.
I want to be excited about
the eighth grade, but because
of the pain, I cannot
concentrate.

Teachers' words
sWiSh and sLuSh
in my ears and then
swim away.

I can barely answer
questions or hold my
pen to write.

My eyes burn and blur
when I read a few pages
or have to focus on
the light from the projector
or the tablet in my face.

I ache if I sit
in my desk for too long
or have to take
the stairs because
they haven't given me
an elevator key
yet.

When I walk the halls
my body churns and chugs

like a rickety roller coaster
at the Galveston County Fair.

In classrooms, the AC air
LoCkS my joints
and ThRoBs under my skin.

Teachers won't let me
stand or move around
too much because it's
a "distraction."

And even though Mami
and Papi told the principal,
the counselor, and my teachers
that I have JIA,
none of them really
understand my DiS-eAsE
and they think that I'm
making excuses and
won't let me leave to call
my mom so I can go home.

So usually, between third
and fourth period,
I go lie down in the nurse's
office.

When I do not get up
by lunch, the nurse calls
Mami to come
pick me up.

TOUGH

When I am able to go to school
and make it through the day,
Maria Tere protects me
like I'm made of glass or ice.

She helps me in and out of my chair
and up and down the stairs.

She lets me lean on her when
I feel weak and she even went
with me to the office when
I told the principal about a boy
who called me a freak.

Behind her back, people also
say things that are mean; still, she
struts through the halls like
she's the queen.

She's been bullied before, for
"dressing like a boy." But
Maria Tere's tough, she doesn't
let anyone steal her joy.

At least not in any way
that I can see

DELILAH

Maria Tere's
made a new friend,
a new girl who moved
here from Houston.

Her name is Delilah Mackin.

She's strong and long and
plays basketball.

Maria Tere's always at
Delilah's locker. Talking
and laughing and trying to
shock her with the latest
gossip, rumor, or joke.

When Delilah laughs,
Maria Tere looks like
she could float.

FAMILY MEETING PART I

One Saturday night, during
dinner, in the middle of August
when the house is sticky
and hot from the humidity and salty air,
Papi calls a family meeting.

There are usually only two
reasons Papi will ever call
a family meeting:

1.   When someone dies.
2.   When he's about to leave for a long time.

Mami has not mentioned
anyone being sick
except for me, and I'm not dead.
So that must mean that
this family meeting is about
the next worst thing
that could happen.

This is not about death,
this is about a different kind of leaving.

FAMILY MEETING PART II

Papi clears his throat.
He tries to smile, but his lips quiver.

Mami looks down at her plate
like she already knows
what he's about to say.

Matti slurps his spaghetti
and bounces uP and DoWn
in his chair.

The air in the room wraps
around my neck and all
I can do is hold my breath
and wait for Papi to break
my heart again.

But this time, it feels even
worse because ever since I got sick
nothing ever seems to stay the same.

FAMILY MEETING PART III

Papi finally speaks:

So I know this isn't the best time,
but you know how it goes,
I don't really get to choose,
and well . . .
they've given me new orders.
I'll be leaving for four weeks
at the end of the month
on a Coast Guard cutter.

GOOD TIME

I get up from the table
and rush to the porch
as fast as my limping
legs can carry me.
Papi follows me out
and hugs me tight.

Papi: *I'm so sorry, Ani.*

He rocks me back and forth.
I cry and cry.

Me: *It's not fair.*
Please don't leave.
My birthday is coming up
and I need you right now.
I'm still not better. And you
haven't even talked to Mami about
swimming and . . .

I cry and cry.
He strokes my hair.

Papi: *I'll still be here for your birthday.*
And, we can talk about swimming
when I get back. It's going to be okay.
You're a strong girl.

I cry even harder because
I don't want to be strong.
I want to be allowed to be
sad and weak and maybe

even give up.
But I don't say that.
Instead I pout.

Me: *It's not fair. Why do you have to leave?*
Why now?

Papi: *I know. I know it is not a good time.*

Me: *There is never a good time*
for you to leave.

SERENITY

Later that same night, Mami comes
into my room and asks me
how I'm feeling. When I pull
the covers over my head and grunt,
she sighs and plops down
on the bed next to me. She pulls
the covers down and speaks slowly.

Mami: *You can be sad that Papi*
is leaving. I am sad too.
This is never easy for any of us.
But you need to accept it. There
is nothing any of us can do
to change it. Ven. Sit up,
and pray with me.

She closes her eyes. (I do not)
She clasps her hands together (I do not),
and she prays. (I listen)

Mami: *God grant me the serenity*
to accept the things I cannot
change, the courage to change
the things I can, and the wisdom
to know the difference.
Amen.

She exhales and smiles as if
that one prayer could magically
make all my despair disappear.

The only thing that prayer
made me feel was what I already
knew to be true: I can't change any
of the things I wish I could.

LET'S GO

Wednesday evening,
after I've already missed
three days of school
due to joint pains and fatigue,
Mami is back in my room.

She pats my leg and shakes
the sheets loose off me.

Mami: *Okay, enough is enough. Get up
and let's go. I want you to go to
youth group tonight.*

I GrOOOOOaaaaNNN and wrap
myself back up like a burrito.

Mami snatches the covers off my face.

Mami: *You may not be able to sit in class
all day, but you need to find the strength
to sit with God. Los jóvenes del youth group
son buenos. You need good friends
in your life.*

Me: *I have Maria Tere . . .*

Mami: *You know what I mean. Now,
get up, get dressed. Maybe
some fresh air will do you good.
Let's go.*

But the only place I want to go
is back to sleep.

YOUTH GROUP

I do not like going
to youth group
because the youth group
leaders all talk too much
about what we're NOT
supposed to do
and how we're NOT
supposed to act
and what we're NOT
supposed to say
and how we're NOT
supposed to dress.

Too many NOTS
got me all tied up.

SLOW

Because I spent so many days
lying in bed, my body is stiff and sore.

I limp into the youth group meeting
room and I can feel my joints rubbing

and bumping against each other like
metal against concrete—a blistering pain

that makes my knees buckle.

When the girls in youth group watch me
walk across the room, they ask me why

do I move so slow, like a sloth?

I tell them about my DiS–eAsE and they
snicker and sneer.

They tell me their nanas and abues have
walkers and canes I could borrow.

I DECIDE

Maria Tere
is the only "good friend" I need
because the girls from youth group
are not the kind of "good friends"
Mami thinks they are.

MEAN GIRLS

The girls in youth group
wear long skirts
and absolutely no jewelry.

The girls in youth group
don't believe in makeup
or shorts or anything
too "revealing."

The girls in youth group
gossip and snicker
whenever they want.

The girls in youth group
say it's probably my fault
I'm sick because I'm not
baptized in their church
and I haven't accepted
Jesus as my savior.

They say I'm the one
to blame and maybe if
I was "saved," God wouldn't
punish me this way.

The girls in youth group
pretend to be innocent
and sweet around adults,
but they torment and torture
everyone they meet.

The girls in youth group
use the Bible and Jesus
to act like they're better
than me.

But I don't think the girls
in youth group know what
being a good Christian
actually means.

MORE DECISIONS

After a few
youth group sessions,

I decide
to tell Mami that I
do not want
to go to youth group
anymore.

I decide
to tell Mami that I
do not want
to go to church
anymore.

I decide
to tell Mami that I
do not want
to pray for
serenity, courage,
or wisdom
anymore.

But then after services
one Sunday,
I hear her talking
about me.

She and la hermana
Dolores are sipping
café con leche
and nibbling pieces

of pan dulce outside
the choir hall.

Between sips of
coffee, Mami gushes
about how she's so proud
of the "good girl"
I'm becoming.

She says she can
already see how youth
group is changing me
for the better.

She brags about how
her prayers are
working and she knows
El Señor
will heal me with
His hands.

So, I swallow
my want and
as usual,
I decide not to tell her
what I want to
tell her.

TEXTING: BIRTHDAY PLANS

Maria Tere: *Hey! What are your birthday plans this weekend?*

Me: *Sunday dinner, remember? Ur coming right?*

Maria Tere: *Of course! But what are you doing SATURDAY?*

Me: *Nothing. I guess.*

Maria Tere: *Ok, don't make any plans. I'm taking you to the beach!*

Me: *Hmmmm. IDK how my mom will feel about that.*

Maria Tere: *Don't worry about her. I've got it covered! See you Saturday birthday girl!*

Me: *Ok! See you!*

THE BEST GIFT

Maria Tere says we're going to search
for seashells like we used to when
we were little.

And even though it sounds like a childish
thing to do, I haven't been to the beach
in months, and I'm ready

to feel the sand between my toes and the water
against my feet. Maria Tere knows being near
the water is the best gift I could ever receive.

And when Madrina asks Mami if she can
take me and Maria Tere to the beach
on Saturday to celebrate my birthday,
Mami says yes because I've been "so good
about going to church and youth group."

Mami says yes, as long as Madrina can
promise not to let me swim and as long
as we make it home before sunset.

SATURDAY MORNING

I dig through the laundry
basket in the pantry to find
my blue beach towel.

Papi's footsteps march, march, march
across the floor in the guest room
next door.

His heavy feet shake the shelves
above the washer.

Papi paces back and forth.

The walls in our house love to carry
sound, so even though he's trying
to whisper, his voice is too deep
and it trembles and echoes.

Papi: *Hi Coach!*

I lean closer to the door and listen.

> *Yes . . . um . . . I'm sorry*
> *I haven't gotten back to you . . .*

My heart begins to pound, PoUnD, POUND
as I wonder what "coach" he could
be talking to.

> *. . . the thing is . . . Ani still isn't feeling well . . .*
> *I know . . . Yes, we were sad she wasn't able*
> *to try out for your summer camp as well . . .*

My face gets hot when I hear Papi
mention "summer camp" because
I remember Coach Leslie was supposed
to attend one of our swim meets
and I desperately wanted to be a part
of Elite Swim Camp.

> . . . *Yes . . . yes, we would love for her*
> *to try out for the winter camp . . . it's just . . .*
> *Oh, there's scholarships available . . . Mmhmmm . . .*
> *Well, we still just need a little more time . . .*
> *. . . to decide . . . her health is our top priority . . .*
> *Please keep a spot open for her . . . Yes, just a little*
> *longer. Thank you.*

A NEW FIRE INSIDE ME

My mind R A C E S, rAcEs, R a C e S
with what Papi could
be hiding from me.

Summer camp? Winter camp?
"More time to decide"?

I StOmP, sTomP, S T O M P
into the guest room
ready to release the fury
of flames suddenly burning
my body from
the inside out.

Papi sees me, sits
on the bed, and buries
his head in his hands.

ANGER

Who was that, Papi?
What do you need to tell me?
What do I not know?

I am a wounded dolphin
thrashing around, bleeding out.

BETRAYAL

Papi: *That was Coach Leslie . . .*

Me: *From Elite Swim Camp?*

Papi: *Yes, she saw your meet back in May.*
She's called before and wanted you try out
     for her summer swim camp.
But you were so sick and now she says
     there's a winter camp too, but . . .

Me: *But what?!*
You said you were going to talk to Mami.
Have you talked to her?

Papi: *No. I haven't found the right time.*

Me: *You should have told me the coach called*
you. Why didn't you tell me?!

Papi: *I was trying to protect you.*

Me: *From what?*

Papi: *From feeling disappointed*
that you couldn't try out.

Me: *I know I wasn't strong enough*
then, but I can try out now,
for the winter camp.
Can't I?

Papi*: I still don't think it's a good idea . . .*

Me: *Why not? I've been feeling better.*
Most days I can walk on my own.
I haven't had a fever and I can tell the
medications and physical therapy are working.

Papi: *I know, mi'ja, but you're still in no*
condition to swim competitively. I think
it's just too much for your body to handle.

MY BODY

Why does everyone
think they know what's
best for MY body?

It is MY body, I am
the one living in it
every day.

Shouldn't I be the one
who decides what MY body
can and cannot handle?

BEACH DAY

Madrina honks her horn.
I grab my things and bolt for the door
before Papi can stop me because
I don't want to talk about this anymore.

When we get to the beach, white sea
foam splashes against our toes.
Maria Tere and me poke at seashells
and hermit crabs in the sand.

Madrina braids my hair and I love
the way her hands stroke my scalp.

She brushes loose curls off my face the
way Mami used to—before she believed
so much in God, before the baby blues,
when she was kind always
and not just sometimes.

Maria Tere draws a sad face in the sand
with a stick and I pick up a plastic bottle
and fill it with salt water.

Maria Tere: *So what's the big deal
about that swim camp anyway?·*

Me: *It's a whole ten days of nothing but
swimming and training. And it's run by
        Olympic coaches and former Olympic
swimmers that are there to help you
        become a better swimmer. And if you
get in once, you can go until you turn eighteen.*

Maria Tere: *That sounds awesome.*
I can't believe he didn't tell you about the tryouts.

Me: *He said he didn't want me to be disappointed.*
     But Papi was supposed to be the one I could trust.
The one who let me be me. But now it seems
     like everyone is against me.

UNDERSTANDING

Madrina strokes my temples
and sings a soft lullaby.
Then she says:

Ani, your parents are doing the best
     they can right now. They are
supposed to protect you. All of this
     is new for them too. Be patient with them
and be kind. Adjusting will take time.

Me: *I guess so, I just don't think it's fair*
*that I have to be so understanding of **their** feelings*
     when it seems like they're not understanding of mine.
I just wish Mami and Papi were as
     understanding as you are about everything.
I wish I could talk to them the way
     Maria Tere talks to you. You didn't even
get mad when she told you she kissed . . .

My voice trails off because
I don't know if I'm supposed to
know what I know.

Madrina laughs.

Madrina: *No, I didn't get mad. Maria*
   Tere is allowed to like or love anyone
she wants. Those are matters of the heart,
   and as long as that person treats her
with respect, yo no me meto en eso.
   But if someone or something was hurting
my Maria Tere, I, like your parents, would
   do everything to protect her.

BUT . . .

Madrina says suddenly,

I do think both you and your papi
            should stop wanting or expecting
for you to return to your "old self."
            Because that's not going to happen.
And that's okay. He and you need to begin
            to accept you as you are.

Me: *But sometimes even I don't know*
who I am anymore.

Madrina kisses my cheek and says:

Mi amor, you are Ani,
   and you are enough, and
            that's all you need to be.

Madrina wraps her arms around
Maria Tere and me and I let her
warm skin soften my sadness.

A FISH OUT OF WATER

Maria Tere smushes wet sand
between her fingers and lets it
ooze out all over our legs.

Maria Tere: *So are you going to try out or not?*

Me: *I don't know. Being out of the water*
is so hard. Every day feels like I'm
drowning on land. My chest hurts
and it's becoming harder and harder
to breathe.

MADRINA'S CONSEJO:

I will not tell you
to disobey your parents,
but—follow your heart.
Just remember, you may break
someone else's when you do.

A LITTLE GIRL

When I get home from the beach,
Mami is folding Matti's laundry.
I plop down on the couch exhausted
from the sun and sand and the heat.

Mami: *How was the beach? Did you have fun?*

Me: *Yeah . . . I guess.*

My voice trails off and Mami
decides to keep talking.

Mami: *Papi told me you had a fight.
He told me about swim camp. And for once he
and I are on the same side about this. We don't think
you're strong enough yet.*

Me: *So does that mean when I DO
get strong you'll let me go . . . ??*

Mami: *Ay, Ani . . .*

Me: *I'm not a little girl anymore, Mami.
I should be able to decide what I get to do
with my body.*

Mami: *You may not feel like a little girl,
but you are still a child, MY child,
and it is my job to protect you . . .*

Me: *Why does everyone keep saying that?!*

Mami: *Because it's true!*

Me: *You're never going to let me*
swim again, are you?

Mami: *I'm just trying to do what's best*
for you.

I lie down and begin to cry.
Without a word, Mami strokes my hair
like she used to when I was a little girl.

SUNDAY NIGHT: MY BIRTHDAY DINNER

The night before Papi leaves
on the cutter with the Coast Guard
is also the night of my birthday dinner.

Mami and Madrina swish their hips
and hover over the stove singing,
stirring, and seasoning all of my
favorite dishes.

Rice and beans boil and g u r g l e
in cast-iron pots. The savory aroma
of pollo güisado swirls through
the kitchen and fills the house.

Tostones get tossed inside a pan that
S i Z z L e S and SpUtTeRs with oil.

The radio plays an endless loop of vintage
Bachata songs neither me nor Maria Tere
know the words to.

Matti runs up and down the stairs with
Aquaman pretending to save the world.

On the dining table, there's a vanilla sheet
cake covered in white buttercream frosting
with the words *Feliz Cumple Ani*
in blue letters.

While we wait for dinner to be ready,
Maria Tere and I play Uno and sneak
little tastes of icing when no one is watching.

¡SALUD!

Before we eat, Papi
raises his glass to make
a toast:

*We have had a rough time
around here lately, but
I have to believe
we are headed toward brighter
days. Ani's health is improving
and I know we'll get
our old Ani back soon . . .*

I sulk down in my seat
and shake my head.
I almost start to cry, but
Madrina squeezes my hand
beneath the table.

I remember what she said
to me on the beach and so
I open my mouth
and say what we both need
to hear:

*No, Papi . . .
I may never really be old Ani
again. And I shouldn't have to
be because I am different now and . . .*

My voice cracks.

Madrina: . . . *and that's okay because*
we all love you and accept all of you
no matter what. Right?

Everyone nods, even Papi,
who hurriedly agrees and says,

Yes, of course, I didn't mean . . .

But his voice goes weak like
a water-logged wooden table
ready to crumble.

Mami takes Papi's hand and looks
up at him like he is her moon.
He smiles at her and brushes
a tear off his cheek.

Papi: *Here's to family, to friends,*
to good times and good health, and
to Ani on her birthday.
¡Salud!

MAY NEVER

As we clink our glasses,
Matti raises his Aquaman
action figure in the air
and screams: *To Aquaman!*

Everyone laughs but me.

Because all I can think
about is how my salud,
my health, and
my life,
may never be the same
again,
may never be Papi's
definition of "good"
again.

LOCKET

After dinner, Papi packs his bags
and calls me up to his room.
He hugs me and his arms wrap around
me like a wave and I wish he would
never let me go.

When he does finally pull away,
he takes a small velvet jewelry box
out of his pocket and places it in my palm.

Papi: *Here.*

Me: *I thought you gave me all my gifts already.*

Papi: *Well, this one is extra special. And
I wanted to save it for last. Go ahead, open it.*

Inside the box is a silver seashell-
shaped locket. Inside the locket
are two pictures. One with a family photo
of the four of us and another of Papi
holding me when I was first born.

Papi puts the necklace on me.

Papi: *Now I will always be close by.*

I hold the locket close to my chest
and cry.

LOVE & FORGIVENESS

Papi: *Also, I wanted to say I'm sorry*
for not telling you about swim camp.

Me: *Does this mean you'll let me*
try out after all?

Papi shakes his head.
And just like that my heart sinks
to the bottom of my stomach again.

Papi: *Let's just give it some more time.*
We can discuss it with the doctor
at your next appointment. Okay?

And I say *okay* because I don't want
to get into another fight.
And I say *I forgive you* because
he's leaving and I don't want
to be mad at him while he's gone.
And I say *I love you* because
he's my papi and I do love him
no matter what.

SEE YOU LATER

Papi hugs me again
and because he does not like
to say the word *goodbye,*
he spins one of my curls around
his finger and whispers:

See you later.

CATEGORY 4: (SHIP) WRECKED

September

DIFFERENT

Things are always different
when Papi is gone.

In the mornings,
the house is quieter
because his heavy feet
don't march, march, march
across the worn wood floors
that shake and wake us up
with his every step.

Mami only plays religious
music and she definitely
doesn't dance in the kitchen.

Matti laughs less and whines
more because Papi is not
there to hold or help him
when he needs it.

Mami sleeps less and
cleans more. And Madrina
comes over every day
to help her with Matti and
keep her company.

But every night after
Madrina leaves,
Mami's nervios always
act up.

MAMI AT NIGHT

When Papi is away at sea,
Mami's midnight terrors
haunt her.

She whispers in my ear that
it's actually because she is
afraid of the tree branches
that tAp TaP tAP against
her window.

Sometimes she stays up late
listening to the floorboards
CrEaK and crickets TwEeT.

She paces the kitchen and
I can hear the CLiCk cLiCk CLiCk
of the gas stove turning on.

That means it's tea time.
I imagine the blue flame billowing
beneath the silver teakettle.
It whistles *eeeeeeeee!!* when
it's ready.

She CliNkS and cLaNks a mug
onto the counter. Then adds
two spoonfuls of sugar
and a splash of milk. She stirs
and stirs and takes one
looooonnnngggg sip.

The front door hIsSsssSeS open.
Her slippers fLiP and fLoP
to the rocking chairs on the porch.
The house is so silent, I can hear
her take a breath.

Mami rocks back   and   forth
back   and   forth until her
cup of tea is finished or
"hasta que le llegue el sueño."

DISTRACTED

When Papi is gone
this time,
I become different too.

I get easily distracted
at school
at home
at physical therapy
at church
in the car
in the shower,
everywhere.

Teachers and Mami
tell me to pay attention
and get focused.

But my mind always
wanders to thinking
about Papi.

I clutch the locket he
gave me, a reminder that
he is not here.

HOW ARE YOU FEELING TODAY?

When my physical
   therapist, Sophie,
      asks me this,
      I want to tell her
  that sometimes
  my mood

    s

        w

   i

       n

   g

       s

like a windchime
  in the rain.

Sometimes I'm so angry
  about the way my legs limp
and my arms ache that I want
  to hurricane everything and
everyone around me.

        Sometimes I'm so confused
          wondering what I did to deserve
      this that the tears come fast
        like a tsunami I can't escape.

Sometimes I'm so scared
  of losing the parts of me
that I always believed made
  ME, that I wish I could board myself
up and shelter from this storm.

Sometimes the sinking ship
            inside me sinks further and
further into my stomach and
            all I want to do is sleep.

But, when she asks,
all I'm ever able to say is:
            I'm fine.

DURING THERAPY

Today, I am slow and rusty.

I raise my arms up and down.
    My knees bob and bend.
        I'm a mechanical crane
            lifting heavy loads
                out of the ocean.

My arms and legs do not
    flex and float like feathers
        like they used to. Instead
            they are eroded sea stack
                rocks ready to collapse.

And this is an improvement.
    I feel a little better than I did
        before, but I don't think it's
            going to be enough to convince
                Mami and Papi to let me swim again.

HOPE

Sophie: *Earth to Ani! Yoo-hoo!*
Are you there? I asked you
to do another rep. You okay?

Me: *Sorry. Yeah, I just got distracted.*
Daydreaming, I guess.

Sophie: *Oh yeah? What about?*

Me: *Swimming.*

Sophie: *Are you a swimmer?*

Me: *Yeah. Well, I was . . .*

Sophie: *Why don't you swim anymore?*

Me: *My parents don't think it's safe.
'Cause of my JIA and . . . other stuff.*

I pause and silently repeat
the words
my JIA, MY JIA.

It really is just MINE
and I can't give it back
or wish it away or put it away
like an old sweater that doesn't fit.

Sophie: *You know, swimming would
actually be really good for you and your symptoms.
You've made some great progress already
and I think swimming would limber
you up even more.*

Me: *Really?!*

Sophie: *Absolutely!*

Me: *Do you think you could tell my mom that?*

Sophie: *Sure!*

AFTER THERAPY

Sophie: *Hi, Mrs. del Mar.*
Ani did really great today in her session.

Mami: *Good. That's good.*

Mami motions for me to follow her out,
but Sophie stops her with her words.

Sophie: *She was also telling me*
that she's a swimmer, and . . .

Mami shoots me a glare.

Sophie: *And I think swimming would actually*
be really good for her joints and her
overall mobility. Exercising in the water
and swimming is something we often
recommend to many of our patients here.

Mami's eyes squint and she huffs.
The (?) curl between her eyes shakes
as she looks back and forth between me
and Sophie as if we were plotting
something evil against her.

My eyes plead with her to say YES.
Say YES! SAY YES!
But she doesn't. Instead she says
the next best thing:

Mami: *Let me think about it.*

My heart swims
            fLiPs
                    FlUtTeRs
                            and D a R t S
                    like a dolphin
            dancing
    with her pod.

SERENITY PRAYER (REVISED)

God grant Mami the **serenity**
to accept that she cannot change me,
the **courage** to face her fears
and let me swim again,
and the **wisdom** to know she and I
are different.

TEXTING JOY

Me: *We have to celebrate!*

Maria Tere: *Celebrate what?*

Me: *My prayers are closer to being answered.*

Maria Tere: *What happened?*

Me: *Mami had a change of heart
    and just might let me swim again!
Sleep over next Saturday at my house
    to celebrate?*

Maria Tere: 👍

Me: ❤

ON CLOUD NINE

For the next few days
I have a pep in my step
and for once
it's not because
of my limp.

FACETIME

How wa—ph-i-cal
the–py? Papi cuts in
and out of the call.

Connection is bad.
When he's out at sea, he can't
get a good signal.

Sophie said I should
swim and Mami said maybe!
Can you convince her?

You owe me that much.
Papi knows I'm still upset
about elite swim.

He smiles and nods.
I pro—ise, to do m— best.
Any—ing for y—
Re—ember to ha— patience.
Good things co— to those who wai—.

WAITING

Later that night,
while Mami waits for sleep
to find her, she calls Papi on the cutter.

Since I cannot sleep either,
I hear her on the phone.

Mami: *Hola, mi amor. ¿Cómo estás?*
No . . . ya sabes. Can't sleep . . .
    I miss you too. The kids are fine . . .
ahi mas o menos. I'm sure Ani told you already . . .
    Yes . . . her therapist says the water could help her . . .
But what if she's not ready?
    What if it actually makes her worse?

I hear Mami put her phone down
and pick up the teakettle.
She puts her phone on speaker.
The water runs.
The gas stove cLiCk, cLiCk, cLiCkS on.

Papi: *But what if it makes her happy?*
 And that helps her feel better?

Mami: *But what would happen to ME,*
if something happened to HER?

Papi: *Something is already happening to her, Patti,*
and neither of us can stop it.

TUESDAY NIGHT

At three in the morning,
            Mami wakes up screaming.
                        Mateo! Mateo! Mateo!
                                    I snap up in bed,
                                                my heart pecking
                                                            inside my ribs,
                                                a trapped hummingbird
                                        desperate to get out.
                        I wobble to her room
                    and whisper at the door,
            Mami, are you okay?
            I peek in and see Mami
        with her arms wrapped
    around Matti. *Sshh, sshh,*
está bien. She rocks
    back and forth and squeezes
        a fist full of Matti's hair
                between her fingers,
                    presses her nose against his ear,
                        and breathes him in and out.
                                    The water.
                                                There was so much water.
                                                And I couldn't save him.
                                    She rocks back and forth.
                        I snuggle up next to her
                in the bed and wrap a blanket
            around the three of us
        as if it were a shield
        or a turtle shell
    and make wishes
on the shooting stars
        streaming down
                Mami's face.

I CLOSE MY EYES AND MAKE A WISH

I wish,
     I wish,
          I wish,

Mami's
nightmares
would end
and she could find
happiness
again.

THE NEXT MORNING

The kitchen smells
like maple syrup and
cooking oil.
Steam rises
from the scrambled
eggs on the table.

I make myself a plate
and begin to eat.

Matti shovels a forkful
of pancakes into his mouth
and pretends to feed some
to Aquaman.

Mami tells him to stop
playing with his food.
Then she looks at me
and says:

*Ani, I know
what the therapist said,
but I do not want you
in the water.*

My fork CLaTTeRs against
my plate when I
drop it.

Me: *But Mami, you said
you would think about it!*

Mami: *I have thought about it
and I do not think the water is safe.
I will not have you going into the water
in your condition.*

Me: *But Sophie said it was safe!
Sophie said it would be good for me!*

Mami: *Sophie is NOT your mother.
I am your mother. And I've decided
no swimming.*

SILENT TREATMENT

For
days,
Mami
and I drift
past each other
like heavy rain
clouds unwilling to
look at each other, un-
willing to speak to each
other, unwilling to release
the water or the words
that weigh us both
down.

UNDER THE ORANGE TREE

Friday after school,
I sit under the orange tree and watch
the sunlight ripple like water between the
leaves. I reach up and tug at an orange. Two more
fall to the ground with it. Plop! Plop! Some fall on the
grass, others splatter and gush on the concrete. I jab my
thumb into the round head of the one I plucked. It spits a
tangy tart juice into my eye that stings and burns. Matti
snatches the orange out of my hands and begins to p u l l
and RiP its skin off with his teeth. He bites into the
orange as if it were an apple. His mouth drips with
sticky sweet orange juice. He sLuRpS and sucks.
I lean in to wipe his chin, but he
pushes me away.

UNFAIR

Me: *Matti, what's wrong?*

Matti: *Why are you mad at Mami?*

Me: *Who said I was mad at her?*

Matti: *She did.*

Me: *I'm mad at Mami because*
    I want to swim and she won't let me.
And I don't think that's fair.

Matti: *But you tell me that I can't always*
get what I want 'cause life isn't fair.

Me: *Well, that's true. I guess.*
Sometimes. But this is different because
Mami is being really unfair right now.

Matti: *Well, I think you're making Mami*
sad and that's also really really unfair.

Me: *No, it's not unfair because I'm*
sad too and everyone just wants me to
*understand how **they** feel and no one*
tries to understand me. And I'm sick and tired
of all of it.

I toss a half-rotted orange at
the fence and it splatters.
Matti winces.

Matti: *That's not nice, Ani. And Mami says God wants us to be nice.*

Matti plops an orange in my lap
and walks inside without
another word.

ONE PERSON

I sit alone on the porch
and wonder:

Is there not one person
in this house who is on my side?

I used to be able to count
on Matti for hugs and love.

And now even he has
turned against me.

ANOTHER FACETIME WITH PAPI

Me: *I wish you were here.*
Maybe you could change her mind.

What I Don't Say:

I won't be swimming
at all 'cause Mami's nightmares
have ruined my life.

She doesn't care what
will make me happy. She's let
her fears control her.

And I'm the one who
suffers the consequences.

Papi: *I'm sorry, Ani.*
I wish I there was more I could do.
I know I've said this
before, but let's give it time.

What if I don't have
time to wait for her to change?
What if later is too late?

Even when I speak,
I still don't get what I want.

SLEEPOVER

I begin to feel better
when Maria Tere comes over
Saturday to stay the night.
Even though there isn't
anything to celebrate now,
we listen to Selena
and Celia and it makes me
feel better.

She jumps on my bed
and I bounce and toss
my head and my curls
side to side.

Our fingers and lips
are sticky with rocky road
and mint chocolate chip.

Our cheeks burn and ache
from giggling and smiling
so much.

Maria Tere helps me forget
for a few moments
about what Mami has taken
from me again.

I paint her nails purple
and gold like her favorite
basketball team.
She brushes my eyelids
with ocean-blue eyeshadow,

We build a fort with my pillows
and blankets and light it up
with the flashlight from
our phones.

In the yellow light we write
our deepest, darkest secrets
on our palms.

OUR "SECRET" HANDSHAKE

Ever since we were little,
we made a pact never to
talk about whatever we wrote
on our hands.

We write whatever secret
we're too afraid to say aloud.

No questions asked.
    No judgment passed.
        No laughing
            or snickering allowed.

When we open our hands
and open our eyes, we
read what the other has written.

Then we spit in our palms
and shake
      shake
        shake
until the secrets

are smudged.
Until the secrets
are gone,
never to be mentioned
again.

SECRETS REVEALED

After we write our secrets,
we close our fists,
we close our eyes,
then
    1
          2
              3
                    OPEN!
Maria Tere's hand reads:

I think I'm in love with Delilah.

My hand reads:

Sometimes I wish Mami were dead.

REGRET

The minute I show
my hand to Maria Tere,
I regret writing it
down. I don't wish Mami dead.
I just wish she'd let ME live.

I BREAK OUR PACT

I ask Maria Tere a question
because I don't want her
to ask me about my secret,
and because I'm really
curious to know more
about hers.

Me: *So you like, **love** love Delilah?*
Delilah from basketball?

Maria Tere: *We promised*
    no questions
             no judgments!

Maria Tere's voice cracks
like an egg dropped
on the floor.

She huffs and turns
away from me.

She hugs a pillow
close to her chest as if
to trap her secret back
inside her.

Me: *I'm sorry.*
    I'm not judging you.
I just never would have guessed.

Maria Tere: *Why not?*

Me: *Well, she's so . . . so . . . girly.*
   And you're not.

Maria Tere: *What's wrong with that?*

Me: *Nothing. You're just so different
from each other, that's all.*

FILL

A loud silence fills
the room and we don't
say anything for a while.

I listen to the crickets
chirping at the moon
outside on the porch below.

I think about how they
are not afraid or worried
about singing their songs
as loud as they want to
and I am jealous of their courage.

I don't want Maria Tere
to ever be afraid of saying
whatever she needs to say.

Not to me.

I am supposed to be
the one person
she can say anything to.

I take a breath and make my voice
soft like the inside
of a seashell
she'll want to fill
with her words.

I ask her another question.
One I think, or at least hope,
she'll want to answer.

ORANGE FANTA

Me: *So what do you like
about Delilah?*

Maria Tere turns
and lies on her back.
The pillow between us
no longer traps
her secret inside.

She looks up at the
glow-in-the-dark stars
on my ceiling and her eyes
g l i m m e r
the way they do when Delilah
smiles or laughs.

Maria Tere's thoughts
drift toward those stars
and her voice sounds
weightless and free.

Maria Tere: *I can be myself around her.*
And she makes me laugh.
    And she's really good at basketball.
And she's really easy to talk to.
    And when I see her, something inside me
bubbles up and sizzles like the fizz
    from an orange Fanta
when you first pour it into the glass,
        you know?

But I don't know,
because I've never
been in love before.

HERE FOR YOU

I play with Maria Tere's
hair and she closes her eyes.
I tell her:

You can be yourself around ME.
    You can always talk to ME
about anything.
    I'm always here for you.
Even if I'm sick.
    Even when I can't get out of bed.
I can still listen.
    I'm still here for you.

Maria Tere opens her eyes,
then looks up at the ceiling.
Her eyes drift off
to some floaty "in love" place.

Maria Tere: *I know.*
And you're a great friend.
Like the best friend in all the world.
And I wouldn't change that
for anything or anyone.
It's just different with Delilah, that's all.
I can't really explain it.

Me: *Oh . . .*

I stop playing with her hair
and sink into the bed,
her words tossing around
and around in my head,
making a mess of my feelings.

LOVE

I want to hate   Delilah. Delilah,
who can make Maria   Tere laugh. Delilah, who
is easy to talk to. Delilah, who makes Maria Tere's heart
bubble and fizz. Delilah, who might replace me as Maria
Tere's best friend. I may not "like" Maria Tere the way
she says she "likes," or "loves," Delilah, but I do love
Maria Tere, like a sister. Like a best friend. Like the
one person who knows me better than anyone
else and I don't want to lose her the way
I've lost everything else. I want to hate
Delilah. But it's hard to hate
someone who makes
your best friend
happy.

ALONE

The first real words Mami finally
says to me come on Sunday morning:

Get up, you're going to youth group.
No te vas a quedar en esta casa sola.

So I go to youth group, and as usual
I sit in the back and say almost nothing.

The girls in youth group still stare
at me when I walk in the room,
but at least they don't ask me any more
questions or talk to me about
their abuelas.

This week, the youth group leaders
talk about a community service project.

One of them mentions something
about the beach and my mind drifts off.

I clutch my locket, stare out
the window, and daydream about
swimming.

I don't notice that the meeting is
over until one of the leaders waves a flyer
in my face and snaps me out of
my daydream.

Youth group leader: *Hey Ani!*
Did you get a flyer?

Me: *Um . . . no.*

Youth group leader: *Sorry about that,*
I guess we didn't see you back here.

I take the flyer, roll it up, and walk
out of the room.

Youth group is just another place
where I get to feel ignored and alone.

NON APOLOGY

On the car ride home from church,
Mami notices the bright blue
flyer on my lap.

Mami: *That looks like fun.*
You should do it.
I think you'll enjoy being
near the water.

I take a moment to actually
LOOK at the flyer the youth
group leader handed me.

It has big bold font on the front,
seashells, turtles, trash cans,
and plastic rings line the border.

The flyer reads:

COME CLEAN UP THE BEACH!
HELP GOD'S CREATURES
AND FIND YOUR PEACE!

But what Mami doesn't understand
is that NEAR the water is not
the same as IN the water.

MARIA TERE ON THE COURT

To get my mind off
my own problems,
Maria Tere invites me
to her next Monday night
basketball game.

And of course I say
    YES!
because I love watching
Maria Tere on the court.

DriBbLe   CrOsSoVeR

   SHOOT!

SpIn   BOUNCE

   LaYuP!

p a s s   JuMp   SHOOT!

Maria Tere on the court
makes three two-point
shots almost all in a row.

Maria Tere on the court
is fast and furious.
She is a cheetah on the run
who cannot be caught.

Maria Tere on the court
is weightless on her feet,

a sliver of incense smoke
s l i t h e r i n g,
    SpInnInG,
            s l i p p i n g,
through anyone
and anything that tries
to get in her way.

ALIVE

When Maria Tere
makes a three-point shot,
Madrina and me
are a symphony of
HOOTS
    HoLlErS
foot StOmPs
    F lAiLiNg arms
and ScReAmS
that may make me ache
in the morning
but right now,
I'm too excited to even care.

Let's go, Maria Tere! Let's go!

When Maria Tere
is on the court
it reminds me of
how I am in the water,
    a creature at home
        in the zone
UNSTOPPABLE.

When Maria Tere
is on the court,
I remember what it's
like to be agile
        athletic
    alegre
and alive.

CATEGORY 5:
(STORM) SURGE
October

SCHOOL ASSIGNMENT

Sitting through classes
has gotten a bit easier now
that my body has adjusted
to the medications.

I can spend
more time at school
and I actually enjoy
being able to focus
and work on assignments
again.

So in history, when
we're asked to write
a biography about a lesser
known historical figure,
I'm excited about
the assignment
because I immediately
know who I'm going
to choose.

ANIANA VARGAS: MY NAMESAKE

Revolutionary
    environmentalist
        protector of the water
           and the Earth,

you were exiled from Quisqueya
    for disagreeing with and
        leading a resistance against
           the Dominican dictator Trujillo.

You were fierce and fought
    for freedom and clean water.
        You rejected rules
           that harmed you or others.
                You trained and taught soldiers
                    who refused to stay silent.
Aniana Vargas,
    Madre de las aguas,
        I promise to live up to your name.

Learning more about your life
    is giving me the strength and courage
        to speak up, act, and take control of mine.

BADASS

Maria Tere: *Wow,*
I had no idea
you were named after
such a badass.
Makes sense though,
because you're as much
of a badass as she was.

Maria Tere gives me
a hug before she leaves
to catch up with Delilah
before next period.

I realize that Maria Tere
is right,
I am a badass
and because of that,
I don't have to wait
for someone else
to help me
or be my hero.

I can save myself.

But there's only one
way to do that.

I decide I'm ready
to do what I have to do
to live up to my namesake.

SERENITY PRAYER (REVISED—AGAIN)

God grant me the serenity to accept
that I cannot **change** Mami's mind,
the courage to try out for swim camp anyway
(because I don't want to **wait** to be happy anymore),
and the wisdom to know that this will
make things **different** between us.

NEW ANI

New Ani will never be "Old Ani" again.

New Ani is learning the difference between
physical and emotional pain.

New Ani knows new words like *auto-immune*
and *idiopathic*.

New Ani is learning when to keep quiet and
when to speak.

New Ani knows this is her body and she can
decide what to do with it.

New Ani is learning that she is strong enough,
like Galveston, to survive storm surges and seasickness.

New Ani knows her life is not like other girls'
her age.

New Ani is learning that it's not just her
body that has changed.

A PHONE CALL

Me: *Hello?*
Coach Leslie?
This is Ani.
Yes, Aniana del Mar.
I'd like to schedule a time
to try out for winter swim camp.
No, my dad is out of town.
He told me to contact you.
Yes?
    Yes . . .
Yes!
    Next week?
Perfect!
    See you then!

TEXTING MY ACCOMPLICE

Me: *I need your help next week.*
I'm trying out for swim camp.

Maria Tere: *Your mom changed her mind?*

Me: *No . . .*
I'm trying out without her permission.

Maria Tere: *Is that a good idea?*

Me: *Are you going to help me or not?*

Maria Tere: *Of course. What do you want me to do?*

Me: *Cover for me.*
I'm going to tell Mami that I'm helping
you and Madrina at the gift shop
after school next Wednesday.

Maria Tere: *What if she comes looking for you?*

Me: *She won't. She's distracted with*
church stuff right now. Some big volunteer thing.

Maria Tere: *And what are you going to do*
if you actually get picked for camp?

Me: *IDK*
I'll cross that ocean when I get there.

VOLUNTEERS

Monday night, the boys
in youth group ask us to hush.

The girls in youth group
groan and huff.

As usual, I sit in the back
and don't make a fuss.

The boys in youth group
say they are in charge of beach
cleanup and they need volunteers.

The girls in youth group
raise their hands and flutter
their lashes all flirty.

I'm annoyed by the girls'
immaturity.

The boys in youth group
say they need people
who are willing to get their
hands dirty.

The girls in youth group drop
their hands, scrunch their
noses, and roll their eyes.

I think again of where my name
comes from and how Papi
says I should carry it with pride.

The boys in youth group
beg, plead, say *come on, guys.*

The girls in youth group
decide to handle snacks.

I finally raise my hand and
volunteer to pick up, collect,
and sort recyclable trash.

PEACE OFFERING

After dinner that night,
I help Mami clear the table.
The rain pounds on our roof.
The house rattles and hums.

It's the peak of hurricane season
and even though this storm
is not a hurricane, it is
still hot and heavy,
angry and loud outside.

Matti hides under a blanket
on the couch and squeals
every time thunder rolls
through the walls
and rattles the floor.

As I sort the trash from dinner
I tell Mami that I volunteered
to help at the beach cleanup
hosted by the youth group.

She stops sweeping and
tucks the (?) curl behind
her ear. Her eyes shimmer
the way water does
when the noonday sun hits
its surface.

Mami: *I'm proud of you, Ani.*

She smiles and looks at me
the way she used to when
I was still her little girl.

ON THE DAY OF THE TRYOUT

My heart quivers and sings like a hummingbird.
My hands dart and dance from one thing to another.

My head swirls and spins like a whirlpool in a lake.
My breath stutters, stops, and gets caught in my chest.

Mami watches me flit and flutter and she asks me what's wrong.
Mami senses I'm hiding something, she just can't prove it yet.

MUSCLE MEMORY

To calm my nerves
and relax my muscles,
before I leave for the Y,
I fill the bathtub
with as much water as it
can take and I slip in.

I let the water
cover me like a blanket.
I hold my breath and count—
    one,

         two,

              three.

Ready, set,
        D

            I

                V

                    E!

I imagine my arms
S a i L i N g and s l i c i n g
through water.
Breaststroke
    Backstroke
          Freestyle.
              Butterfly.
                  F L Y!
I may be out of practice,
but I know
my muscle memory
persists.

WIND AND WATER

I believe that sometimes
good things come
to those who act.
I hop on my bike
and head to the Y.

I take my time
because I don't want
to tire myself out.

My legs and arms
feel limber after the warm
bath, but I want to save
my energy for swimming.

I only pedal when
I have to and the rest
of the way I let

gravity pull me forward
and down.

And when I can,
I close my eyes and
g   l   i   d   e.

I pretend the wind
in my face is water.

When I finally arrive at the Y
I know I won't have
to pretend much longer.

A RAY OF LIGHT

Coach Leslie sees me walking
into the pool area at the Y.

She waves me over and flicks
her long blond hair over her shoulder.
Her arms open like petals to greet me.
She pats me on the back and beams.

Coach Leslie is an Esperanza flower—
bright, warm, and filling me
with hope and yellow light.

Coach Leslie: *I've waited so long to meet you.*
Your win at the May swim meet
was impressive.

My face flushes red.

Me: *Thank you.*
I haven't been swimming in a while.
I'm a little rusty.
But I promise I'll do my best.

Coach Leslie: *I'm sure you'll do great.*
Honestly, this is a formality.
I knew I wanted you to be a part of
camp the moment I saw the precision
of your breaststroke and backstroke.
Your form is exquisite, Ani.

WARM-UP

Shower and swimsuit.

Goggles and cap.

Towel and watch.

Lunge and squat.

Circle and bend.

Breathe in and out.

Focus and stretch.

TEXTS I DON'T SEE

Maria Tere:
Ani, where are you?
If you see this text me back.
Your mom just called me!

Maria Tere:
I think your mom knows!
She asked a lot of questions.
Ani, text me back!

Maria Tere:
Your mom is at the gift shop!
Wants to know where you are!
What do I say?

Maria Tere:
Ani, I'm sorry,
I had to tell the truth.
She's on her way to you.

BEFORE I DIVE INTO THE POOL

I watch the hands of the clock on the wall
slide the seconds away.

I inhale and the sharp smell of chlorine creeps up
from the water and cuts my nostrils.

I exhale my fear and doubt into the starting block
beneath my feet.

I steady my breath.

I listen to the splish splash of swimmers in nearby lanes.

I shimmy my shoulders, bounce my knees, and feel
fluid and flexible.

I adjust my goggles and pull down my swim cap.

I feel others' eyes on me.

I wait for Coach Leslie to count down
and tell me to   GO!

BUT BEFORE I DIVE INTO THE POOL

Mami
makes
landfall
and
her
heels
thunder
across
the concrete:
Aniana
del
Mar
bájate
de
ahí
y
ven
aquí.

EVACUATE

It's too late to run.
Hunker down. Board up the windows.
Pray someone will save
me from this storm. Watch, as the
water rises beneath me.

WATCH

Other people's eyes
dart back and forth between
us as they watch the whole
scene unfold.

In my ears, their whispers
and gasps become
tornado winds ready to
swallow me up.

THE EYE WALL

Mami StOmP, sToMp, StOmPs
over to the edge of the pool
where I am in position
ready to p L u N g E.

Mami is all thunder and lightning,
a threatening hurricane
made of hot water and high tides.

Mami PuLL, puuuull, P U L L S
me up and yanks me
off the swimming block.

A whirlwind of questions
and complaints circle, slice,
and swallow me up.

Mami: *What were you thinking?*

     Why do you disobey me?

         Have you not learned your lesson yet?

             How dare you betray me again!

Mami ShAkE, sHaKe, SHAKES
her head and heaves a heavy sigh.
A torrential rain   p

                o

                u

                r

                s from her eyes.

MAMI'S EYES FLOOD ME WITH

her fear
    her fire
        her prayers
            her past
            her turmoil
        her torment
    her wounds
her worries
        her loss
        her longing
            her love
        her sorrow
    her storm
her rain
    her thunder
        her fight
    her flight
her fear

WHAT IF

Ani,
what if
something happened
to you?

What if you drowned?

What IF
no one was there
to save you?

REALIZATION

What Mami fears
is not the water.

What Mami fears
is losing someone
else she loves.

What Mami fears
is the guilt that comes
when you believe
you are the one to blame
for someone else's
death.

PLEADING

Me: *Please—*

This isn't fair . . .

   Please—

The doctor said swimming would help . . .

   Please—

It's just water and I know how to swim

   Please—

Look at me. I'm fine. I feel fine.

   Please—

ATTEMPTED RESCUE

Coach Leslie: *What seems to be the problem? Why can't she try out?*

Coach Leslie tries to stand
between me and Mami.

But she is no match
for Mami's storm surge.
Mami's strong arm pushes
her out of the way like debris
caught in a tunnel of wind.

Coach gets tossed aside.

Mami hisses at Coach:
> YOU *stay out of this.*
> > *Ani es mi hija*
> > > *and I decide what is best.*

Mami usually uses her words
to hurt, but today she's using
her whole body.

I have never seen her like this.

STILL PLEADING

Me: *Mami, don't be like this . . .*

> *Please—*

Just let me try out and you'll see . . .

> *Please—*

I am not me when I'm out of the water . . .

> *Please—*

Let me be ME.

> *PLEASE—*

MORE WHAT-IFS

Mami: *Ani, no. What if*
I lost you too?

What would happen
to ME
if I lost you too?

Me:

Mami,

what

IF

this

isn't

about

Y
     O
          U?!

DIRECT HIT

Just when I think
    it can't get
         any worse,
             one of Mami's
         praying hands
     StRiKeS
my soft cheek
    and I wobble
        like a seaside
            house crushed
      by a hurdling wave.
    Someone catches
me before I fall
      to the floor.
        Tears pool in
            my eyes,
       My face floods
     with warmth.

THE HOLD

It is not easy to love
a hurricane mother
who wants to swallow you
up in her ocean arms.

It is not easy to accept
that your mother's fears
are an ocean
drowning you out.

It is not easy to understand
how the mother who once
held you with love
is now the storm
striking you
down.

(BEACH) CLEANUP:
Still October

HEAVY

Inside our house
hangs another heavy silence.
It weighs down the walls and floors.
Like a syrupy moan
or a thick groan.
It's like nothing
I've ever heard before.

But maybe that's because Mami
has never hit me before.

Mami stays in her room
and I stay in mine.
Our doors and mouths stay shut.

Without a word,
Mami cooks, cleans, and most days
walks right past me as if
I'm not even there.

I read, sleep, go to school
and physical therapy,
come home and read
or sleep some more.

Matti scurries between us
like a mouse afraid of getting
caught in a trap.

FACETIME: LESSONS

Papi:
I heard what happened.
Why didn't you tell me
about tryouts for swim camp?

It didn't have to
be this way, Aniana.

Papi hangs his head.

Me:
I know you're mad at
me, but this is your fault too.
From the beginning,

I wanted to tell
Mami. You are the one who
made me keep secrets.

UNDUE STRESS

Doctor Castro has told me
that stress can "aggravate"
my JIA.

Doctor Castro has told me
that even though my JIA
can be managed, "undue stress"
on my mind or body could
cause a "flare up."

Which means
that my symptoms
can come back full force
and make me feel as bad
as I did before.

AFTER

After the incident at the Y during my failed tryout,

after Mami screams and shouts,

after Mami says *no phone, no swimming, no afterschool activities,*

after we don't talk to each other for days and days,

my body and my mind can't seem to handle the stress

of all this pain and silence and sadness,

and even though I was feeling "fine" before,

my symptoms begin to flare and nothing feels fine anymore.

FLARE-UP

My   sadness

creeps   under

my   skin   and it   BURNS

my body   from the inside out.   Every morning

when I wake   and every night   when I try to rest,

my joints   SCREAM   and   BEG   for the sadness

to GeT OuT!   But my grief   has nowhere to go   like an ant pile

that's been stepped on   and destroyed   my sorrow   s c a t t e r s

over   and under   every part of me   and even if I found   a wa

to d rrrrr aaaaa gggg   it out   I'm not sure   I would know

where to put it.

TEXTING: GUILT

Maria Tere: *You know I'm sorry, right?*
About telling your mom.
About it being my fault.

Me*: It's not your fault.*
It's mine.
Everything is my fault.

Maria Tere: *No it's not.*

Me: *Then why does it feel like it is?*

A SWEET TREAT

Matti brings
me an orange from
our tree and plops it onto my lap.
I know Mami says we're not supposed to eat
oranges in bed, because they make a mess, but if you
don't tell her I won't. Matti blinks twice because he
hasn't learned how to wink. I want to warn him
about secrets. How secrets are slick and sneaky
like water. How secrets will surge and suck you
up like a whirlpool or a heavy rain. How
secrets will slip through your fingers and
soak and soil everything you love if
you're not careful.

ALTERNATIVE MEDICINE & MORAL SUPPORT

Maria Tere and Madrina
come to visit and they bring
ginger tea, caldo, Florida Water,
and peppermint oil for my aches and pains.

Madrina and Mami fry
plantains and gossip in the kitchen.
Matti builds towers
and knocks them down while
Maria Tere and me curl up
on the couch with blankets and watch cartoons.

We sip tea and snack on crackers
while we wait for the soup
to heat up on the stove.
Maria Tere rubs the peppermint
oil on my knees and elbows.

Maria Tere: *Are you going to
that beach cleanup event this weekend?*

Me: *I don't know.*

Maria Tere: *Well, if you DO go, I'll
come. For moral support.*

Maria Tere winks and nudges me gently.
I roll my eyes and crack a smile.

Me: *Oh no, if we go, you're
definitely helping!*

LAUGHTER IS THE BEST MEDICINE

Then, Matti begins to hop
from the couch to the floor pretending
to be a superhero. When he lands
on the floor for the third time,
and just as Mami is about to tell him
to STOP,
he FARTS!

Everyone in the room
begins to laugh.
Even Mami.
Even me.

We laugh until the tears
come out of our eyes.

We laugh until Madrina
realizes the plantains
are burning.

We laugh so hard we don't
even care about the smoke.

We laugh so hard our
bellies hurt.

And suddenly I notice that
my other aches and pains
are just a little less painful.

EARLY SATURDAY MORNING

It is still dark
and the full moon hangs
bright in the sky
like a clock on a wall
telling time
by how clearly you can see it.

A thick fog coils
around the trees and
houses on our street
like a fragile white
caterpillar cocoon
that could stretch or break
with the slightest touch.

I try to settle in bed
after another night
of little sleep because
the thoughts in my head
won't stop, when Mami
comes to my room and
tells me to get up.

PROMISES

Mami: *The beach cleanup is today.*
   You volunteered, so get up
      and get dressed. Matti and I
         will wait for you downstairs.

Me: *I thought I was grounded . . .*

Mami: *You are, but this is the Lord's work.*
                    And you've made some bad choices
                          lately, so maybe this can be your way
                    of starting to turn things around.

Now get up.
     Tienes un compromiso, and it's
                not good to break your promises.

And who knows, maybe the ocean
     air will do you some good.

ANOTHER NON-APOLOGY

I'm surprised Mami
WANTS me to go to the beach.
Is this her way of
saying *I'm sorry* without
having to really say it?

Maybe Mami does
feel bad that she took away
the one thing I love.

THE OCEAN AT SUNRISE

Strokes of pink and blue
    wisp above the water
        like bubblegum cotton candy
           at a carnival.
               The ocean's static hum
           drowns out all the other
       noise stirring inside me.
   All I can hear is the ocean
asking me again
    to make a wish,
          wish,
             wish.
                My muscles relax,
            my joints soften and
        it seems as if my sadness
      is fast asleep.
  The sea-salt air sinks
deep into my skin and
    flutters my lashes.
        My curls skip across
           my cheeks like a feather
             or a leaf on the ground.
         I dip my toes in the sand
      and scrape my feet along
         the water.

FRIEND-SHIP

The girls in youth group
hand out bottles of water
and bananas.

The boys in youth group
organize recycling bins
and hand out gloves and
trash bags.

Maria Tere locks her arm
with mine. I lean my head
on her shoulder and sigh.

Me: *I'm glad you were able to come*
with me today. I know you'd rather
be sleeping.

Maria Tere rests her weary head
on my head and whispers in my ear:

You're my best friend in the whole
wide world. I'd do anything for you.
Even if it means waking up
at the butt crack of dawn when I've
stayed up late the night before
texting Delilah.

I smile,
grateful
that our friend-ship
is the one ship in my life
that has never sank.

THE PARTS WE PLAY

Mami and Madrina
set up a table and help
the girls in youth group
hand out
    water bottles
           bananas
                and apples.

Matti and his ball
sit in the sand near
Mami's feet.

He builds a sandcastle
then destroys it
        bOoM!
             POW!
              BaNg!

Maria Tere and me
pick up and sort,
pick up and sort,
bottles
    cans
        plastic
            and paper.

The waves wax and
wane and it seems as if
the ocean is trying to say
      thank you
           thank you
              thank you.

CLONE

Walking down the beach,
with bags of trash in our hands,
Maria Tere finds a sand dollar.

She picks it up, inspects it,
and says:

Look what I found.
    It reminds me of you.

Me: *How?*

Maria Tere: *In science class, we learned*
                that sand dollars clone themselves.
                    In self-defense.

And that's kind of what you've
    had to do. You know?

You've become another version
    of yourself in order to stay alive.

Me: *Thanks. But I don't want to be praised*
for just existing. You know?

Maria Tere: *Yeah . . . I get that. Trust me,*
I do.

Me: *Managing my illness*
doesn't make me brave. This is just my
way of living my life now.

Maria Tere: *Wow. When did you get so wise?*

I smile and shrug and we keep
walking and picking up trash
and little treasures, leaving
the beach a little better
than we found it.

DISTRACTION

Then,
in
a
s   p   l   i   t
second
when
Mami
leans
d o w n
to pick
up
a bottle
of water
from
a cooler,
Matti's
ball
r   o   l   l   s
away
and
he
r   u   n   s
into
the
ocean
to
grab
it.

SLOW-MOTION SCENE

Mami screams:

Matti! ¡Ven aquí!

But Matti keeps running
in
in
in.
Matti! No!

The waves lift and crash against
him
him
him.

Matti! Please God! No!

The waves topple, drag, and surround
him
him
him.

Matti!
Matti!
Matti!   *Come back!*
Mateo,
Mateo,
¡Ay mi Mateo!

BOLT

Mami's
screams
pierce and
shoot and
split through
my spine like
a lightning bolt
that slices the
night sky with
silver light. These
are the ugly screams of her nighttime terrors.
These are the screams that haunt her like the
ghost she can never seem to forget. These are
the screams that
shake and wake
her grief, that
flood her when
she remembers
who and what
she lost so
long
ago.

IN THE DEEP

I turn back
    toward her echo.
        Mami runs into
            the rush of waves.
                She flails and flounders
            like a seagull with a
        wounded wing. I look
    back and forth between
Mami and the water.
    The deep water that would
        always make Mami say
            That's too far.
                The deep water where
            the sun glistens and glosses
        over the surface like glass
    but never cuts to the bottom.
The deep water where Matti
    lifts and lowers
        lifts and lowers his head.
            Where Matti gasps
            and grasps,
                gasps and grasps
                    for air.
                Where Matti
        steadies, then slips,
        steadies, then slips
    into the deep.

INSTINCT

All I see
behind my eyes
are Mami's
screams,
the color
of fire.

I

           d
               r
                    o
                         p

my bag.
KiCk off
my shoes
and I

             r   u   n

and J U M P
            in
                   in
                        in.

RISE WITH THE TIDE

I have not been held
by the ocean and her
warmth in months.

I have not used these
legs and arms to swim
since my body began
to burn.

I have not held
my breath underwater
in so long.

But my body remembers
what it's supposed to do.

I slice and swim through
the waves with ease.

I do not resist the ebb
and flow. I lift my arms
and rise with the tide.

I pray:
Aguas del mar—
do not betray me now.

I remember:
    I am a dolphin.
                I am Ani
    de las aguas—
I can do this.

LIFEGUARD

Mami always said
it was my job to
protect Matti.

And so I guard
him with my life
and p u l l
                P u L L

                          P U L L

him out of the water,
confused and coughing
but still breathing.

SWEETNESS

I
squeeze Matti like
an orange I want to burst.
I kiss his face and neck, smell
his soft sweet skin, and taste the
salt water that stains his cheeks. He
wiggles away. And for once, he
asks me an easy question I can
answer: *Ani, did I drown? No,
Matti. You didn't drown.
I got you. I got you.
You're safe.*

A MONSOON

We are coated in sand
and salt water. The sun
warms our skin and pulls
our eyes shut. A crowd
of people clap.

The girls in youth
group say:
Amen. Amen. Amen.
The boys in youth
group hoot and holler.
Maria Tere and Madrina
ask: *Are you all right?*
        Are you all right?

When I open my eyes,
I see Mami pushing past them all.

She's a monsoon
of lagrimas y lamentos.
Tears and tristeza
streak across her face.
Her knees buckle.
Her arms swoop in
to hold us.
She collapses on top
of me, a broken wave
of sorrow and regret.

RECONCILIATION

Mami sobs:

Ay mis hijos.
I'm sorry.
For everything.
I'm sorry.

I whisper:

>*I'm sorry too.*

Matti mutters:

>*Me too! I'm sorry too!*

We laugh
and Mami wraps
her arms
around us
and cries.

Her prayers
answered.

(RE)BUILDING:

November–December

FACETIME: MATTI'S STORY

Every time I try
to talk to Papi, Matti
interrupts us and

takes my phone to tell
Papi the story of how
he almost drowned and

I rescued him from
the waves and the sharks and whales.
Papi always laughs

and listens closely
as if it's the first time he's
heard Matti's story.

As if I really
did save him from sea creatures
and waves made of flames.

PRIDE

Papi calls and when I am able
to take the phone
away from Matti
I tell Papi:

I miss you.
        And I can't wait
                for you to come home.

Papi says:

I am proud of you.
Not just for saving Matti,
but for who you are.
For the young lady you're becoming.
For the strong and brave
warrior woman who I know will
always live up to her
name.

HERO

Since the beach cleanup,
I have received messages
from many people

who said that what I did
was so heroic and brave
and I should be proud.

And I am proud of myself
for jumping in to save
Matti, but I wasn't trying
to be anyone's
hero.

I just did what felt right.

DELILAH, MARIA TERE & ME

Lately Delilah, Maria Tere, and me
sit together every day at lunch
to talk and eat.

This is where I learn
a lot about Delilah and it helps
us become friends.

I learn that Delilah
is not only a basketball player,
but she's also into competitive diving.

I learn that she loves the water
as much as she loves the court
and when she's not talking
to Maria Tere about basketball
teams and sports, she shows me
videos of Olympic divers
on her phone.

I learn that Delilah's mom
is also in the Coast Guard and
she leaves a lot like Papi.

But Delilah is an only child,
which makes the leaving feel
a lot more lonely.

I learn to like Delilah and I love
our lunches together
because it turns out Delilah
and me are more alike
than different.

(TALK) THERAPY

Mami has always said she doesn't believe in talk therapy.
But after what happened, Madrina tells Mami:

Why don't you practice some of what your Bible teaches?
Reconcile. Find the courage to make things better
between you and Ani.

Reluctantly, Mami eventually agrees.

So now, once a week, Mami and I go to an office,
sit on a couch, and talk to a therapist.

We talk about our anger, our sadness,
our hopes, and our frustrations.

Sometimes we cry. Sometimes we laugh.
Sometimes we pray. Sometimes we get angry.
Sometimes we don't know what to say.

The therapist reminds us:

It's important to talk to each other instead of
bottling it up inside.

It's important to realize healing takes time.

SWIM TEAM

During one of our therapy
sessions, I choose to live up to
my namesake and I find
the courage to ask Mami:

I know I missed the deadline
for winter swim camp tryouts,
but can I return to swim team
at least?

Mami sighs and says she still
isn't sure if she's ready
for me to join swim team again.
BUT
She says: *We'll see. I'll talk*
it over with Papi when
he returns.

And instead of getting mad
or sad because she didn't say yes
I say:

Can we ALL talk about it
together and decide?

Mami reaches for my hand:

Claro que sí.
We can even call a family meeting
if that's what you need.

WHAT WE MISS

The therapist says it's important for
Mami and me to have fun together.
So the week before Papi returns
Mami takes me again to the nail salon.

Even though we talk a lot in therapy,
while we sit in the massage chairs,
and women rub our feet,
Mami and I talk some more.

I ask her about growing up
on her island.
Mami says what she misses most
are the sounds of the city streets
buzzing by her bedroom window
and fried chicken from a place
called Pica Pollo.

She asks me about school
and what I loved so much
about swim meets.
I tell her I miss waiting
with my friends for my heats
and the wonderful feeling
of winning a race.

A BOLD MOVE

In a bold move, Mami decides
to paint her nails Caribbean-Ocean
blue for Papi.

Then, while the nail tech layers on
one last coat, Mami grabs my hand,
squeezes it, and says:

Perdón, mi'ja.

Me: *For what?*

Mami's apology catches me
by surprise because things have been
good between us, so I'm not
sure why she's apologizing.

Mami: *For how I treated you at first,*
when you got sick. For believing
> *that your illness was God's way*
of punishing you for keeping secrets
> *and lying to me. For blaming you*
for your illness.
> *I understand now,*
that's not how God works.

HOW GOD WORKS

Mami: *They say God*
works in mysterious ways,
and I believe that.

We may never fully understand
why you have JIA.
Just like I will never understand
why my Mateo was taken from me.
But I'm learning to accept
all of it.

And if all of this has taught me
anything it's that I also believe
God works in loving, kind,
and forgiving ways.

And from now on, I want
to work at being a little more
God-like.

BETTER: A HOMECOMING

When Papi returns
the house is louder
and livelier because Papi shouts
HELLO! and *¡BUENOS DIAS!*
when he enters a room or
wakes up in the morning.

His big belly laugh echoes
through the halls of our house.
His quick feet carry Mami from
sadness to salsa dancing,
even when she says she
doesn't like it.

Mami smiles more and sleeps
through the night because
her bed is not as cold as it was
and she knows Papi is safe
in her arms and not out at sea.

Matti giggles and squeals
because he has Papi to run and
tumble and roughhouse with.

And I no longer need to miss him
because not only is Papi close
to my heart inside my seashell locket,
he is also sitting right here
next to me.

SHOW & TELL

We show and tell Papi everything
he missed while he was gone.

Matti points to his elbows
and knees and shows off his scars.

Matti: *I got this one from falling off*
my bike. And I got this one from falling
off the monkey bars.

I share my Aniana Vargas biography.

Me: *Everyone loved it! I even got an A*
and they displayed it in the hall for a whole week!

Mami shows off a new skirt and tells Papi
everything she's been learning in therapy.

Mami: *The therapist says it's important*
to say what you're feeling, when you're feeling it.
And not bottle it all up inside.

Papi wraps his arms around
Mami's waist and smiles.

Papi: *You want to know what I'm feeling right now?*

Matti squeals: *What? What?*

Papi: *I feel like the luckiest man in the world.*

LOVE

On Sunday
we all go to church,
even Papi,
to give thanks
for his safe return
home.

We get dressed
in our Sunday best
and I feel so good
I'm not even worried
about the hard wooden
church pews.

At church I sit between
Mami and Papi
and listen closely
to the sermon.

The pastor recites
a verse that tells us
love is patient and kind.
Love does not get angry
easily and it keeps
no record of wrongs.
Love always protects,
trusts, hopes,
and perseveres.

When I think about
our family
and everything we've

been through,
I know that's exactly
the kind of love we have
for each other.

And suddenly *I* feel
like the luckiest girl
in the world.

FAJITAS & A FAMILY MEETING

After church we pick up
fajitas and virgin margaritas
to go from Tortuga's.

We take it home and spread it
all out on the dining table.

After we eat and laugh
and Papi finishes telling us
all his stories about his shipmates,

I tap on my glass and ask
for everyone's attention.

Papi's eyes get wide.

Papi: *Wait a minute, who died?*
    What's going on?

I laugh and shake my head.

Me: *Nobody died. I just have something*
    I want to say.

I take a deep breath
and even though my palms
are sweaty and my heart
is racing fast, I let the words out
and ask what I want to ask.

Me: *Can I please go back to swim team?*
And this summer can I try out for swim camp?
I feel a lot better and I promise I'll be safe.
It would mean so much to me! Please?!

ON THE SAME TEAM

Papi sighs out in relief,
then he looks back and forth
between Mami and me.

Papi: *I think that if you feel strong enough,*
I'm okay with it. As long as you take it slow
and tell us if your symptoms flare
and you can't handle the grueling practices.

I run around the table
and hug Papi tight, then I look
at Mami and wait for her reply.

Mami: *I agree with your father.*
We're finally on the same team. You can go back
to practice and join the team again.
But I don't know how I feel about a week
away at swim camp. Let's discuss THAT
in a few months. And aside from what Papi said,
I have two more conditions . . .

I hop up and down and squeal.

Me: *Anything! I'll do anything,*
what are the conditions?

Mami: *You still have to go to youth group.*

I groan and grit my teeth.

Me: *Fiiiinnneee . . .*

Mami: *And no more secrets, lies, or hiding anything.*
If there's anything else you haven't told me,
      now is the time.

Mami looks back and forth
between me and Papi and suddenly
I remember that there IS
one more thing.

TOOLBOX TREASURES

I rush to the garage
and pull out my medals
from Papi's toolbox.

I take them to the kitchen
and lay them all out
on the dining table
      one by

            one

                  by one.

Me: *These are the medals I've won*
and I hope one day you can
watch me win more in person.

Mami's eyes fill with water
and she hugs me tight,

                          tight,

                                 tight.

The warmth of her arms,
is the greatest treasure
I could ever receive.

MATTI'S QUESTION

Matti stands on his chair
and screams:

Ahem! Ahem! Excuse me!

Papi tells him to sit down
but he doesn't listen.

Matti: *I want to call a family meeting!*
I want to win medals like Ani,
    so I have a question.
Which one of you is going to
    give me swim lessons?

Mami and Papi look at each other
briefly, then in unison they point
at me and agree:

ANI!

GROUP TEXT

Me: ☺ ☺ *OMG guess what?*

Maria Tere: *What?!*

Delilah: *What?!*

Me: *Papi AND Mami said . . .*

Delilah: *Said WHAT?!*

Maria Tere: *SAID WHAT?!*

Me: *I can rejoin the swim team!*

Delilah: ♥ 🎉

Maria Tere: 🎉 ♥ ☺ ☺

MATTI'S FIRST LESSON

I walk with Matti
into the shallow end
of the pool.

Mami sits right by the edge
with her feet in the water
holding a towel
and a life preserver in her arms
"just in case."

She keeps telling me
to be careful
      be careful
            be careful
as she whispers
soft prayers under
her breath.

Papi sits next to her,
holds her hand, and
assures her:

They're going to be fine,
you'll see. Ani is the best
swimmer. She knows what
she's doing.

I carry Matti to a deeper
end and then I have him
lie facing up.

I keep my hands under
his back and I tell him
the first lesson in swimming
is about trust.

I tell him to trust me.
I tell him to trust the water.

And when I finally
move my hands away
and let him go, he
F L O A T S.

BEFORE THE MEET

After weeks of demanding
practices, it's finally time
for my first meet of the new
swim team season.

Before the meet, Madrina
finds me in the locker room.
She hugs me tight and pulls
a small stone from her pocket.

Madrina: *Here, I want you to take it.
And don't worry, I asked your mother
already if it was okay.*

I take it and hold the smooth stone
in my palm. I stroke its
round edges with my thumb.

Me: *What kind of stone is it?*

Madrina: *It's a black bloodstone
crystal. It can bring you good luck
and endurance.*

I hug Madrina and we take a
deep breath together in and out.

Me: *Thank you, Madrina. Not just
for the stones, but for never expecting me
to be anything other than what I am.*

REPRISAL: INDIVIDUAL MEDLEY

I make my way next to
the swimming block
and the first person I see
and hear in the stands
is Papi.

He is already screaming:
Ani!
      Ani!
            Ani!

Mami, Madrina, Matti,
and Maria Tere
are all in the stands
with him.

Mami keeps closing
her eyes to pray.

Matti waves his Aquaman
doll up and down
in the air.

Maria Tere smiles at me
and I give her a thumbs-up.

She and Delilah begin
to whistle and cheer
even before I step onto
the starting block.

I hear the whistle.

I get on the starting block.
I adjust my googles
and take a breath.
Papi coaches me
from the stands:

Ani Aguas, remember
        don't fight it.
Find your rhythm
and g l i d e,
      s Li D e,
              FLOAT.

Mami points at me:
¡Esa es mi hija!

Her joyful scream
the beautiful medley
I've been waiting to hear.

Take your marks!

I close my eyes
make a wish—and wait.
Then the whistle blows.
                1
                        2
                                3 . . .
                                        I jump in.

★ ★ ★

(DEL)FIN

AUTHOR'S NOTE

Dear Reader,

Thank you for choosing to follow Aniana's journey. While this is a work of fiction, Aniana and I share many things in common. For example, she and I are both Dominican American girls living with chronic illness and disability whose fathers are or were in the military. However, I made some deliberate choices while crafting Ani's character in order to ensure that her journey was unique and authentic to the story I wanted to tell.

For starters, why is it set in Galveston? Texas has been my home for almost twenty years. And it holds a special place in my heart. I knew I wanted Ani to live near the ocean, and I knew the metaphor and imagery of hurricanes and storms was going to be central to the story. Galveston, being one of my most favorite places in Texas (I even got married there and we visit a few times a month), seemed like a natural fit. The city has a history of enduring and surviving devastating hurricanes and flooding. I wanted Galveston's resilience and strength to serve as a metaphor for the various storms Aniana encounters in her own life.

Aside from choosing a very specific setting, I was also deliberate about the names of my main characters. In all of my written work I try to honor and pay homage to famous or noteworthy Dominican and Dominican American women. One of the ways I do that is by using their names for my characters.

In this book, Aniana del Mar (Aniana "of the ocean") is named after Dominican revolutionary and environmentalist Aniana Vargas (1930–2002). Vargas, better known as "The mother of the waters," was an anti-Trujillo political activist and a defender of environmental conservation. Trujillo was a ruthless dictator in the Dominican Republic for over thirty years and Vargas worked with political activists to try to take him down. Because of her activism, she was persecuted and exiled from the island.

Another one of these anti-Trujillo activists was María Teresa Mirabal (1935–1960), who Maria Tere is named after. Mirabal was one of four sisters who secretly plotted to assassinate Trujillo but were eventually caught, jailed, and then assassinated by his men.

Both Vargas and Mirabal risked their lives to take down Trujillo and restore freedom and democracy on the island. It is my hope that you will be inspired to learn more about them and the work they did.

Lastly, I want you to know that this story was inspired by own journey with chronic illness and disability. Like Ani, I was diagnosed with an auto-immune disease that disrupted my life and my dreams. At the age of twenty-two, just a few days before my college graduation, I was diagnosed with scleroderma.

Scleroderma, like JIA, is a chronic, auto-immune disease that affects the skin, joints, and other vital organs like the heart, lungs, and kidneys. I chose juvenile idiopathic arthritis as Ani's illness because scleroderma in children often manifests differently than the way I experienced it: I felt I had a better understanding and connection to JIA based on how similar our symptoms are.

I was not as young as Ani when I was diagnosed, but I still had many dreams and goals that were paused after my diagnosis. In college I studied theatre and had hoped to one day move to New York and become a Broadway actress. But having scleroderma changed that. Acting, rehearsals, performing, and even just teaching theatre became too difficult.

Because of my debilitating symptoms, I, like Ani, had to give up doing what I loved most for some time. But unlike Ani I did not fight for it. I remember feeling lost and confused. I remember feeling alone and scared. I thought for sure my life was over and I wanted nothing more than to be my "old self" again. While Ani also struggles with these same feelings, I wanted her to be more courageous. I wanted to give her an agency, or a sense of control over her own life and journey, that took me a long time to find.

If you live with and manage an illness or a disability, I hope that you see yourself in these pages. I hope that Ani's triumphs bring you joy and that her story helps you feel a little less alone. If you do not live with a chronic illness or disability, I hope this story shows you how to be kind to everyone around you because you never know what someone is going through. We are all fighting silent battles the rest of us know nothing about.

A NOTE ABOUT POETRY

This book uses several poetic forms you may be interested in exploring. I encourage you to see if you can find these forms in the book, and give them a try for yourself!

Concrete/Shape Poems: A poem where the words are arranged into a shape or pattern that may reveal an image related to the poem's subject or theme.

Haiku: A short form poem that originated in Japan. Haikus traditionally have three lines and seventeen syllables organized as follows:

Line 1 (5 syllables)
Line 2 (7 syllables)
Line 3 (5 syllables)

Tanka: A short form poem that originated in Japan. Tankas traditionally have five lines and thirty-one syllables organized as follows:

Line 1 (5 syllables)
Line 2 (7 syllables)
Line 3 (5 syllables)
Line 4 (7 syllables)
Line 5 (7 syllables)

GRACIAS

Every book is a labor of love. Every writer begins their story-telling journey alone, but along the way, if she is wise, she will ask others to join her. Aniana's story was my idea, but it would not have been possible without the support, guidance, patience, and love of many people.

First and foremost, I want to extend a bigger than Texas thank-you to my agent Stefanie Sanchez Von Bortsel at Full Circle Literary. Thank you for believing in me and saying yes to this story after reading only the first twenty pages. Thank you for supporting and championing my wild and special dream of writing a novel in verse about a chronically ill Afro Latina girl from Galveston. Thank you for introducing me to Nancy Mercado, my editor and guiding light during the revising and editing process. Nancy, thank you for mothering my characters and this story in ways that I never could. Thank you for asking the difficult questions and pushing me past my comfort zone.

Thank you to my ancestors, my grandparents and my parents. Thank you, Mami, for being there for me when the offers came in and I started to cry in disbelief. Thank you for saying what I needed to hear: "Tú te mereces esto y mucho más." Thank you, Papi, for giving me my love of books and for teaching me with your actions that it's never too late to pursue your dreams.

Thank you to my father- and mother-in-law, Pedro and Eusebia Mendez, for always treating me like a daughter and welcoming me into your lives seventeen years ago. You have always made Galveston feel like home, and that is why Ani lives there. Ani's story would not exist without you.

I began writing *Aniana* in late 2020, weeks after my mother-in-law, Eusebia Mendez, passed away, as a way to hold space for and process my own grief. During that time, my immediate family, found family, community, and friends showered us (me, my partner, Lupe, and our daughter, Luz Maria) with so much love and grace that I will never forget it.

Thank you to the many communities of writer friends that I am a part of. I appreciate that I can count on so many of you to answer my questions and humor my rants, frustrations, ideas, good news, and rejections in the group chats.

Before any book sees the light of day, it must pass through many hands. I'd like to thank my early readers and critique partners David Bowles, Addie Tsai, Camryn Wells, and Gris Muñoz for your kind and generous feedback when this story was just a seed. Thank you to my sensitivity reader Alaina Lavoie for your kind words about my work and for pushing me to see Aniana in her wholeness.

Mil gracias also goes to all of the folks behind the scenes that turn our stories into physical books the world can hold. One in particular that I'd like to acknowledge is artist and illustrator Gaby D'Alessandro for rendering Ani and parts of her story on the cover of this book so beautifully and authentically. Thank you also to editor Rosie Ahmed and copyeditor Regina Castillo, and to my cover designer Danielle Ceccolini, and to Jenny Kelly, the designer of the interior pages, for taking the time and energy to ensure all of the poems were shaped and formatted correctly. I know it was no easy task.

Thank you to the patients, families, and medical care providers who live with and treat JIA, like Emilio J, Lugo who provided insight into what it's like to be a swimmer living with with JIA. Your stories inspired this one and I hope it helps you feel a little less alone. Thank you also to my rheumatologist Dr. Shervin Assassi, for answering my questions about JIA and for always asking me "how is the writing going" at every appointment. You have saved my life in more ways than I can count.

I would not be where I am without my partner in poetry and in life, Lupe Mendez. You have always put my needs first. You have always made sure I had a room of my own to write, work, dream, and do yoga in. Thank you for helping me make these dreams come true.

And, lastly and most importantly, thank you to the one human who has brought the brightest light into my world. The little girl I wasn't sure I'd ever get to meet. The one who makes it all worth it, and who I hope sees herself in all the stories I write. Thank you to my life, my love, my everything Luz Maria Magdalena. Every day you teach me how to be a better person. Every day you remind me to find joy. I am grateful for you in ways you do not understand yet. Mami te quiere mucho, mi'ja.